The First Draft

HONEY HOLLOWAY

Copyright © 2025 Hayley Anderton

All rights reserved.

To the love of my life. I'd be lost without you.

OTHER BOOKS BY HONEY HOLLOWAY

All books are available to purchase as paperbacks or ebooks.

Break Me Gently: A Best Man Romance Novella
All My Monsters: A Poetry Collection

CHAPTER ONE

Oliver

At some point when you join university, you discover that making it to a nine am lecture is nearly impossible. Not because students don't own alarm clocks; this morning, I've pressed snooze at least five times, waking up a little more angry each time the alarm rings. And it's not because we don't care that our money's going down the drain, either. Deciding to go to university is like deciding to use all your life's savings on an epic night out. It feels good before you do it and during, and then afterward, it makes you feel like you've made a terrible mistake. So yeah, we care that we're watching our money being drained from our bank accounts, but we still don't make it to nine am lectures. Why?

Because we're all lazy as fuck.

At least, that's the way it is for the Creative Writing students who have made it all the way to the third year of our course. We're all fully aware that going into lectures is a waste of our time. Not one of us can stand to hear another poem by a crappy contemporary poet when we could be dreaming in bed and letting our imaginations do the teaching. I groan as the alarm goes off again, signaling that this is our final chance to make it to class on time.

"Turn it off," Violet moans, her hair sticking to her lip and her eyes screwed closed. "I'm getting up."

"Are you hell!" I say, slapping at the snooze button once more.

"Our grades are going to be fucked…"

"You haven't created a bad piece of coursework since the lecturer got your piece mixed with Brian's. You could've aced this course when you were three. Just close your eyes and go back to sleep…"

She throws the covers off her body dramatically, and my eyes are drawn to her naked body. We've seen each other naked a thousand times during our casual sex agreement, but I've never really taken the time to look at her, somehow. Our encounters always happen in the darkness at night when we're filled with booze and confidence. She stretches her arms above her head and her small breasts seem to disappear into her chest. Her slim body is all protruding bones and acres of pale skin. Her bobbed black hair and honey eyes draw my attention as she blinks the sleep from her eyes and runs her fingers through her hair like a comb. She's gorgeous, of course. Any man would be lucky to wake up next to her. But to me, she's just my best friend. Sometimes, when I take the time to look at her like this in the morning, I wonder why we do it. It's never complicated things between us so far, but it's like an addiction. It's only hard when you try and stop.

"You know, you shouldn't be so sure of yourself. You know half of this course is about kissing the tutor's asses," she mumbles bitterly. "Just because you're a class favorite when you bother to show up, it doesn't mean it'll stay that way. If you don't start going to the lectures and seminars, you'll fall behind."

"Then stop taking me out clubbing every Tuesday night…"

Violet rolls her eyes and I laugh at her, grabbing her waist and pulling her back into bed. Now that we're sober, touching her naked skin feels more forbidden, but I want her to stay. I'm in the mood for more of what we had last night. My hand ventures between her legs and I tease her with a grin. Her body relaxes in my arms and she closes her eyes, letting out a soft gasp. She's already wet.

"You know you want to stay," I murmur playfully in her ear. "We don't need to be anywhere. The world is putty in our hands, Violet."

She tuts at me, but she doesn't even open her eyes, enjoying the feeling of me touching her between her legs. "You have the privilege of that opinion, Oliver. You're a rich foreign student. You came here with nothing to lose…"

I want to laugh at that comment. She doesn't have a clue how much it really took to get me here. But I decide instead of arguing to finish her sentence.

"…and we have nothing to gain if this course is anything to go by….come on, Violet. You know it's a waste of our time." I clamber on top of her, my hand still between her legs. She finally looks up at me, a small smile playing on her lips. I tease her mercilessly with my fingers and she gasps as I work up a rhythm. She never lasts long when I'm touching her.

"Stay here instead...enjoy the moment," I whisper. I lean in to kiss her gently, and it feels a little strange. I'm not used to being so present while we're doing this. I'm usually a little drunk and not really thinking too hard about what we're doing. But Violet grabs the back of my neck to pull me in close and I know she's into it. We're not going anywhere.

She pushes herself against my fingers, forcing them inside her. She's always been good at telling me what she wants. I use my thumb to touch her clit and kiss her neck as I penetrate her with my fingers. I can feel the rise and fall of her chest as she lies beneath me and I feel her satisfied breathing on my neck. This is what we're so used to, and yet it always feels good. I like being with her and not having any strings attached. It's the closest to perfection I've ever found in a sexual relationship.

I can't help feeling aroused. It's always strange being so sexually attracted to the girl I call my best friend, and yet nothing could stop me right now. I pick up the pace and Violet moans quietly. We've mastered the art of being quiet so that my flatmates don't hear.

"You can go now if you want. I won't stop you," I tease her. She laughs, pinching my cheek playfully.

"Yeah, right. It's just getting good…"

"Only just?" I ask her. I trail my lips down her chest to take her nipple in my mouth. Her laughter turns to the sound of her pleasure.

"You can do better than that…" she breathes, though I can tell she's completely at my mercy. I push my fingers deeper inside her and she doesn't bother playing around any longer. She wants what she always wants. A sweet release.

I can hear that she's about to finish and I seal the ending with a quick kiss. She moans against my lips, bucking against my hand one last time. I grin as she reaches out to touch my erect cock, which has been left unattended in our session. With her arousal still on my fingers, I know she's ready for at least another round…maybe even more. She strokes me lazily for a few moments and then she grins at me and pulls away.

"What are you doing?" I complain.

"Going to class," she says brightly, wriggling out from underneath me and standing to get dressed. I stare at her in shock, laughing out loud involuntarily.

"Are you serious? You're just going to leave me hanging like that?"

"It's not my fault you started something I don't have time to finish….besides…I got mine," she says with an innocent smile. She finishes hastily dressing and blows a kiss in my direction. "See you at the writing circle later...if you can be bothered to get out of bed."

"You're the worst."

"And you're the best. Later."

I laugh, shaking my head to myself before burying my face back in my pillow. Even though I wish she'd come back and finish the job for me, I'm not mad at her for leaving at all. This is why Violet and I get on so well. We never expect too much of each other. We always know where our boundaries lie. And we both agreed, right from the start, that things would never become awkward between us. After all, no one is claiming we'll ever get together. No one in our friendship circle is insisting that they see some unspoken chemistry between us and that we're going to be the couple of the century. We're fine as we are, and neither of us has some hidden desire to take it to another level.

Now that I'm alone, I'm completely tempted to go back to sleep, but the moment I shared with Violet has woken me up somewhat. I reach for my laptop, which I abandoned on the floor last night after watching a film with Violet turned into sex. I'm going to force myself to put pen to paper - or fingers to keys - and write something good today.

I'm groggy and tired, but as much as I refuse to go to a lecture right now, I may as well use this time for something useful. I'm lazy, but I'm not unmotivated. I want to succeed in this course, especially since my brother, Caleb, paid for me to come over here. He's always been concerned that my laziness will lead me to a dark pit of depression eventually when I give up on my dreams and start allowing my bad habits to take over. I disagree, but I'm thankful in so many ways that he pushed me to come here from overseas. Sure, this course is killing my passion for writing with each lecture I attend, and sure, it's not the sort of university course that will land me a job right away. But I've found happiness here. I've found friends for life. I've found independence.

And most importantly, I've found an escape from the dark spiral life in California was taking me down.

I take the day as it comes. I spend the morning writing and then get up at midday to drink copious amounts of coffee and eat some slightly stale toast. It makes my hangover seem a little worse so I head back to bed for a nap. When I wake up, I realize I've missed the beginning of my meeting with my writing group and rush out to meet them. No one is surprised that I'm late, and we all joke about the night we spent out at one of Liverpool's worst clubs. Then we get serious and listen to Violet's poetry. It's kind of a perfect day.

By the time I get home, I know it's almost time for my weekly chat with The Bachelors, as I named our group chat several years ago when we went our separate ways across the globe. It's mostly because our last name is Bachelor, but also partly because we're all single as hell. Ezra found himself in a pretty serious relationship for a while, which is completely typical of my crazily romantic older brother even if it ended terribly, so I guess he doesn't exactly love being referred to as a bachelor, but it's a part of our identity whether he likes it or not.

Still, the group name has stuck, and I'm reluctant to change it. It seems like the only constant between us these days, other than our weekly catch-ups. Now that none of us live together and we're all out doing our own thing, it's easy to feel disconnected from them. Once, my siblings were my favorite people in the world, keeping me afloat even when the going got tough. But I guess things have changed a little since our father's funeral.

I wait patiently for the others to join the call. Tammy is the first to show up. She grins at me with a wave.

"Good day to you, young whippersnapper," she says, miming drinking a cup of tea with her pinkie finger in the air. In her mind, the British jokes haven't gotten old yet, but she couldn't sound more different from the people I've met in Liverpool. Violet was born and bred here, and her husky Scouse accent surprised me so much when I first met her that it took me several weeks to get used to. Still, Tammy's energy and enthusiasm always make me smile. She's always been my secret favorite out of the bunch, though I'd never admit that to her. She'd be far too smug.

"Hey, Tammy. How're things?"

She fakes a yawn. "Same old, bro. Mom's been in a good mood this week, though. She hasn't shouted at me once."

My heart aches a little for Tammy. As the youngest, she's the only one still living at home. She's old enough to move out now, but someone's got to look after Mom. I guess the rest of us got out just in time.

"Good to hear. Has she been going to therapy?"

Tammy scoffs. "What do you think?"

I shake my head to myself. Since the car accident that killed Dad and left Mom with mental scars, she's been more like Tammy's child than her mother. Sometimes, the one thing that gets me through is knowing that my third year will soon be over and I can go back to help her out. As much as I don't want my life to revolve around my mother and the mistake she made, it's not fair for Tammy to get stuck either. Especially since Caleb refuses to talk to Mom and Ezra has issues of his own to deal with...

"Alright...and what about you? Are you at least getting out of the house?"

"Dude, you know it. I go out with my friends every night," she says proudly. Her face is clearly showing signs of her late-night adventures, too. She looks pale and gaunt despite her smile and her wide eyes. Her hair is shorn close to her head, leaving nothing to hide the tiredness in her ga\e. But I guess Tammy has always been the master of pretending everything is fine. Even if she is spending her nights drinking and her days making sure Mom doesn't give up on life.

"Good...and you're eating enough? Drinking plenty of water?"

"Woah, dude...just because Mom's not lecturing me about it, doesn't mean you need to. I'm fine, Oliver. You don't have to worry about me."

"It's my job as your big brother."

"It's alright...I've got three of those. And you're the most fun of the three, so maybe you should leave the lectures to them…"

I chuckle, just as I get a notification to say that Ezra is joining the call. Tammy pulls a face.

"Don't mention Leo…"

I put a finger to my lips as a promise. Ezra's ex-girlfriend is allegedly returning from her travels that broke the two of them apart in the first place, so it's safe to say he's going to be in a bad mood. I sigh quickly before Ezra appears. As much as I love them all, it would be nice to see them all smiling.

Ezra's face is so miserable when he appears that I almost laugh. He's let his facial hair grow rugged again, and his thick brows are knotted together. He sighs as a greeting.

"Where's Caleb?"

"Nice to see you too, Ez," Tammy says, rolling her eyes. Ezra shakes his head.

"Sorry...I'm a little distracted today. Leo's coming over to pick up her things in a little while…"

"What? Seriously? It's been almost a year since you guys ended...what's keeping her?" I ask. He shrugs.

"I guess her traveling around Asia had something to do with it. She clearly had better things to be doing," Ezra mutters. We all fall quiet, not knowing what to say. Caleb, for all his flaws and seriousness, is much better at handling this kind of thing. He'd know what to say to make Ezra feel better. But since he's not here, we sit in silence, and I start wondering when things got this hard between us guys.

When Caleb finally shows up, it brings a smile to all of our faces. As much as Caleb is the grump of the family, my eldest sibling is also like the mother hen of us all. When things went to shit at home, he was already well established in his career as a lawyer, and he made sure we were all well looked after. He insisted on paying my tuition fees to stop me from getting into debt. He sends Tammy money to keep her and Mom going, despite the fact that he won't even speak to Mom. He pays for Ezra to have studio time twice a year to record an EP, even though Ezra always struggles to get something recorded. Basically, Caleb is the selfless one among us. Though I guess it's easier to be selfless when you're loaded.

"Everything okay, Ezra?" Caleb asks right away, stroking his chin on his handsome face. He's dressed smartly like he's just come home from work. Then again, he doesn't often leave the house in anything other than a suit. Tammy catches my eye on the screen.

"It's like we're not even here, Olly…"

Caleb sighs. "Well, he's the priority tonight. We spent half an hour last week talking about your night out, Tammy. Have some perspective."

I try to be sympathetic to Ezra. After all, his hopelessly romantic heart is more fragile than most, and Leonora really did a number on him. But it's just a fresh reminder that as much as we all smile and joke around usually, our family is a bit of a mess.

If only I could turn back time and stop the crash from ever happening, maybe things could be different.

Willow

Getting up at six am feels like a lie in today. As I force my eyes open and turn off my alarm, I switch on the light to wake up my body, wincing at the pale lightbulb hanging above me. My shift at the local cafe starts in an hour, but I only finished my last work shift five hours ago. Still, five hours of sleep is a generous amount for me, so I try to be glad of it and psyche myself up for the day.

I rush to grab a bagel and take a shower. I take time drying my hair and applying my signature gold eyeliner. I like to make an effort for work. Since I spend my life either on a shift or studying for university, it quickly became evident to me that if I don't make an effort now, I never will. Besides, it's nice to look nice.

But of course, there are obstacles every morning, and the latest one is that my work shirt has shrunk in the wash. I don't have time to clean and dry my other one, so I guess I'll have to hope my boss likes crop tops. I pull on my black jeans too, sighing at my midriff on show. My wide hips and belly are on display now, making me feel a little naked, but I've never had much shame about my body. The customers will just have to get used to it.

Downstairs, my terrible neighbors are arguing again. I sigh. They're the reason I've taken to sleeping with headphones on. I thought getting a proper apartment instead of student accommodation would be cheaper and less rowdy, but my tiny one-bedroom flat is surrounded by young couples in dingy conditions going just as crazy as I am. I'd be sympathetic to them if they didn't keep me up at night so often.

I check my phone as I'm heading out. I sigh. My freelance employer wants me to do a complete rewrite of the work I submitted. I don't get paid enough to care, and yet I need this job. I can spend a few extra hours on it or I can fail to pay my rent and end up out on the streets. When I think of it that way, the choice seems much easier. I just wish that for once, someone wouldn't take advantage of my situation. Maybe if someone put themselves in my shoes for once, they'd see how hard it is to be twenty-one and fighting to be able to pay my own rent.

The sun is making an appearance as I show up for my shift. Several groggy customers are waiting outside for me to let them in. I put on my customer service face and unlock the doors, allowing them inside to the warmth of the coffee house. I take my place behind the counter, knowing that the other baristas will be at least ten minutes late. They always oversleep and come in with lame excuses about it, but I don't mind so much. The chaos of the start of an early shift makes it go much faster. And considering I'm working until twelve then heading straight to a lecture, I need this to go as quickly as possible.

Two hours in and the early morning commuters fizzle out, leaving me with little to do, but daydream. I wish I was at home right now, tucked up in my bed with my ancient laptop on my lap. I wish I could work on my poetry for class instead of the work I owe my employer. I wish I could enjoy university the way that my classmates do. I'm a social creature, and I'd love to throw myself into partying and extra-curricular clubs, but unfortunately, there aren't enough hours in the day. Living the loner life is the only way I get through the rest of this year. Maybe next year I'll have a shot at a new life.

I lean against the counter, my body tired from being stood up for hours and not having enough sleep. I need to try and look at the positives. I'm going to finish my degree with work experience from my freelancing. I'm going to finish my course to a high standard because I use all my spare time and energy on it. I'm going to be able to get a job right away…

Or at least, that's how I convince myself to continue.

I take out my phone and manage to write a few lines of my short story that's due at the end of the semester. I feel a warmth inside me as I tap away on my screen. There's something about writing first drafts that I love. They're messy, often nonsensical, a splatter of words on a page that don't quite connect. But it's the baseline for something great. There's a reason that writers love this part. It's finding your feet. It's knowing that by the time you're done with it all, you'll have something special. It's enough to keep us going when writing feels impossible. And I love to steal moments away from the mundane to create, to build something outside of the monotonous life I've trapped myself in. It makes everything worth it.

It's moments like this that I can appreciate that my hard work will get me places. I might be alone in my experiences, but me, myself and I will reap the benefits someday. I pay for my rent myself. I've been taking care of myself for as long as I can remember. And someday, those things will matter more. The fact that I haven't gone bankrupt is a miracle. Besides…I might work two jobs now and sleep much less than I should, but I don't think I can ever go back to the way things used to be.

The door opens and I hear raucous laughter. I check my watch and sigh. Right on cue...I know exactly who is at the door.

Oliver and his friends from my course saunter in like they own the place. Oliver has his arm slung around Violet's shoulders and she's looking at him in adoration. I almost roll my eyes. They come as a pair, them two...completely inseparable most of the time. It's like the rest of the group isn't there when they're gazing at each other like that. I've never been a fan of PDA, and it always makes me feel a little nauseous when they show up here on Thursday mornings. Still, Oliver always tips after he buys his coffee. And he always says the same thing to me each time when he comes up to the counter to order…

"Loving the hair, Willow," Oliver tells me with a grin, nodding at my vibrant blue hair. The drawl of his warm Californian accent is one of his saving graces, and it always makes me want to change my mind about how much I dislike him, but I can never be certain of how sincere he's being. "The usual, please."

I nod and turn to use the coffee machine for his and Violet's joint order. I don't tend to be a rude person, but I try to avoid speaking to Oliver each time he comes in here. I can't quite put my finger on what irritates me about him. It's something to do with the way he walks around with the confidence of a man who has everything he could ever want. He shows up late to classes or not at all, and yet he's easily one of the best writers I've met here. In short, he's privileged and it serves as a reminder to me that I'm not. Some people have life handed to them on a silver platter, but some days, it feels like it's people like me who have to keep giving that platter to someone else.

"How're things, Willow? You missed my party last week…"

"I had to work," I tell him bluntly. "You missed class yesterday…"

Oliver smirks. "Yeah, well, I had better things to do…"

"Really? Better things to do than attending the course that's costing you nine grand a year?"

Oliver still has a smile playing on his lips. I want to slap it off him. "My bed was calling me."

I plonk his coffee on the counter irritably. "Some people don't have the luxury of wasting all that money on staying in bed, you know. Nine am lectures suck...but so do the people who think they're above going to them."

Oliver's cheeks turn red and I know I've said too much. I get that he wasn't trying to be provocative...he just doesn't realize how bloody lucky he is. I fetch Violet's coffee for him.

"Eight pound twenty, please."

Oliver gets out his card and a bunch of coins, refusing to look me in the eye as he puts the change in the tip jar.

"You know what, you're right," Oliver says solemnly. "I need to take uni more seriously." He offers me a small smile. "Otherwise I'll never beat you for a space in the magazine."

I blush. Each year, our university publishes a booklet of student's work. Only the very best of the submissions get published, and so far, I've made it into one magazine out of two, despite the fact that it's usually just reserved for third years. There's also a coveted spot for the best piece right at the start of the magazine, and I'm aiming to be the one who snags it. Oliver is clearly hoping this will be his year too, but he's not truly being competitive, I can tell. The worst thing about Oliver is that he's completely irritating, but everyone can tell that he means well. It's hard to hate him when his intentions are never as bad as his attitude.

"Hey, listen...I know I've asked before and you've said no...but you should really join our writing circle," Oliver says to me. "You've got a lot to offer the group...I think everyone could benefit from having you around. Plus, it would be a chance for you to...socialize."

I blush again. So it's apparently clear to everyone that I don't have a social life at all. I bow my head. Part of me would love to join his group. But even though it's only a couple of hours a week, it's a few hours I can't spare. I can't even justify it as work when I know they spend most of their meetings drinking beer and joking about the tutors.

"I think I have to work," I say lamely. What else can I do when my whole life is centered around trying to stay afloat?

"What about my party on Friday then? I'm pretty sure I sent you an invite...everyone needs to let loose sometimes."

I laugh without humor. "Thanks for the concern, Oliver...but I doubt I'll come. I've got a lot on my plate right now."

He nods stiffly. I think he's still a little stung by my comment about him not showing up to class. "Alright, I understand. See you around, Willow."

He saunters back to his table as though nothing just happened, and his friends greet him with their usual bravado and enthusiasm. I sigh and go back to leaning on the counter, watching them subtly as they joke around. It's like I'm looking through a window at the life I wish I could have. And the fact that I've picked myself up out of the gutter doesn't make it an easy pill to swallow that I still don't have everything I want. I know I should be grateful. Even in a shitty flat, I still have a roof over my head. Even working long hours, I'm still able to care for myself with the money I earn. Even though my Dad didn't want me and I have no family, at least I have my health. I'm one of the lucky ones.

And yet, with a glance in Oliver's direction, it doesn't feel that way at all.

Work ends. A lecture begins. Then that ends too and I head home to work on my freelancing. I've got the kind of headache that rests behind your eyes and makes your vision fuzzy, but I work through the pain, telling myself it'll be worth it. As night draws in, a party begins on the floor above and I switch my headphones up to full volume, drowning out the sounds of rowdy drunks. It's just another distraction from what I have to get done by the end of the night.

Next to me, my phone is buzzing with messages for once. The dating app that I signed up for a few days ago caused me to swipe listlessly for about ten minutes and has resulted in a few matches and eager messages from boys in the area. Deciding to give myself a two-minute break, I glance at the messages and I'm instantly appalled. In total, I've received one unsolicited dick pic, one plea to go over to someone's flat for the evening, and one corny joke from a guy who I'm almost certain is a catfish. I roll my eyes and try to get back to work. I don't need a man to be satisfied, after all. I don't need sex or constant company. I just need to feel a little less alone.

I know how this goes. I've been down this route before. I'll spend some time daydreaming of the possibility that someday, someone will love me the way I deserve to be loved. I'll finish work late, but I won't sleep. I'll crawl into bed at three am and wonder how it feels for the lucky ones who curl up next to their partner every night and take it for granted.

For a moment, my mind wanders to Oliver. I think of the way he had his arm around Violet so casually, like their relationship is solid enough for them to stop making an effort. Some part of me is jealous, but I can't figure out why.

Am I jealous of Violet because she has Oliver, or am I jealous of Oliver because everything has fallen easily in his lap once again?

CHAPTER TWO

Oliver

It's early, but I've managed to force myself out of bed today. Willow made me feel pretty bad when I saw her yesterday. I'm fully aware that she thinks she's superior somehow because she goes to her classes every day and performs well on every single task, but somehow, her little comment got through to me. Maybe I shouldn't let her get in my head. I've been doing just fine without her opinions. But part of me knows that she's right, and that only makes me feel more irritated. Not with her, but with myself. She's forced me to really look at my reflection for the first time in a while, and I'm not sure I like what I see. All this partying and messing around is dulling something in my eyes. I roll my shoulders back and crick my neck, preparing myself for the day. If I want a spot in the magazine - and I do, I really do - then I'd better start taking things more seriously. Especially if Willow is my top competition.

I have to admit, there's something about her that really intrigues me. I don't know her that well, mostly because she's never let me close enough to try, but I've always admired her, even if it's clear she doesn't feel the same about me. There's something really cool about her. She's always so calm and collected, so well-spoken and smooth. She's not deliberately cruel or unkind, but she has the ability to make a grown man squirm. She certainly had that effect on me yesterday. It helps that she's so fucking good to look at, with her dark makeup, her tattoos and nose ring, and deep blue hair that only girls like her seem to be able to pull off.

And damn did she look good yesterday. I don't know if it was some kind of fashion statement, but she wore her work shirt short, cut above her stomach to reveal her curves. Violet once made a comment on how girls her size shouldn't wear crop tops and we argued about it for almost an hour. The way I see it, anyone can wear whatever they want. And in the case of Willow, she looks good in everything she wears anyway. Just because she's the polar opposite of a girl like Violet, it doesn't mean she isn't sexy as hell.

I guess it's safe to say she's been on my mind. Last night, I couldn't stop thinking about her, which is something that's never happened before. Sure, she's passed through my mind from time to time, but other than that, Willow stays tucked at the back of my mind until we meet via class or my coffee pitstops. I've liked to keep it that way, knowing I'm not even on her radar.

But last night, I lay alone in bed and thought about what it would be like to have an enigmatic woman like her lying next to me. To touch her, to have the freedom to explore her body, to give in to the desire that I feel when I see her. I imagined the ways in which she'd feel different to Violet, whose slight body beneath mine always feels breakable. I get the feeling that a woman like Willow likes to be in charge, and I can't imagine that I'd mind much if she was taking charge of me.

I was hard for a long time, just thinking of the way her shirt rose up to reveal inches of her pale skin. I tried for hours to ignore the fact that she was turning me on, but my mind kept coming back to her. I eventually fell asleep with fantasies of her in my bedroom haunting my dreams. Now, this morning, I'm rushing off to a workshop that she'll be attending, mostly because I need to start keeping up with my studies, but also partly because I'm excited to see her again. It's dumb. She'll spend the whole day looking through me like I'm not even there. But a guy can indulge in a daydream about a woman every now and then right?

That said, these workshops are the worst. They require us to bring in a sample of our work and share it with the class for them to comment on. Not only do I hate sifting through terrible pieces and finding good things to say about them, but I hate when people are fake with me. Everyone on this course is so desperate to please that they'll tell you anything to keep you on their good side. With the exception of my tutor and Willow, I've never had constructive criticism from anyone in my seminar, and what use is that to me? I might have confidence in my abilities, but I know I have a long way to go to reach perfection.

And today, my very personal piece is being scrutinized by my classmates. It's my worst nightmare, but I've sat through weeks of reading other people's stories, waiting for my chance to get some feedback. Finally, I'll be able to figure out if I'm on the right track, even if the whole process makes me feel sick to my stomach. I just need to keep my confident persona up for the next two hours and then I'll be able to work on getting better. That's the whole reason I'm here, after all.

Everyone else is already seated as I enter the seminar room and my tutor, Sabine, looks up sternly as I enter the room. Unlike some of my other tutors, she's a lot less lax and expects us to at least be on time. She purses her lips as the other ten students stare at me.

"We thought you weren't going to show up, Oliver. We're discussing your piece first. Take a seat. There's a lot to talk about."

There's a free seat next to Willow and Sabine, and my heart skips a beat. As much as I always try to get Willow to talk to me when we cross paths, we've never sat together in class before. When we're in the lecture hall, she sits on the far side of the room alone. But in seminars like these, where the atmosphere is so much more intimate, it excites me to be sat next to her for the first time. I keep my back straight and my chin high as I sit down. Being beside her has added to the butterflies in my stomach, but in the best possible way.

Sabine coughs to get the class' attention. "Good morning, everyone. It's good to see there's a full house for once. Now...anybody want to kick off with a comment on Oliver's story? As always, you should've read it through several times and made notes. Good points and bad are welcomed. Who is starting us off?"

"I will," Willow says right away. She always seems to be the first to volunteer, while with everyone else it's like getting blood out of a stone. Still, it still feels good to have her volunteer. She glances at me with a mere hint of a smile.

"It's a sad story, Oliver. Really moving, and really believable. Reading it back a second time, I felt like I understood the woman in the story much better because you know exactly what she's been through. It's easy to see her as selfish and self-centered after the death of her husband, especially when in some ways...well, I guess you could say it's her fault. But I guess it just goes to show that you don't know a person's background before they decide to tell you about it. It's a classic example of a character holding their cards close to their chest in order to conceal the reasons for the way they are. It's both intriguing and cleverly done. I think it's a triumph."

I can't help grinning at her. I told myself I'd play it cool, but man, she's really shown me the sweet side to her. I feel a twinge in my stomach again, my dreams of her from last night still fresh in my mind now that we're in the same room together. I never expected such good feedback from her, especially after the moment in the cafe yesterday. But the more I smile at her, the more I notice that the corners of her lips are twitching involuntarily too.

And then Sabine goes and ruins it.

"Thank you for starting the discussion, Willow. I think it's safe to say that we all value your opinion in these workshops," Sabine says. The rest of the class stares at Willow in clear irritation but it's true that we'd all be lost without her here.

I turn to Sabine and try to read her expression, but instead of the smile I'm expecting, I'm met with her hardest stare. Usually, she has something positive to say to me, but today, it seems I have disappointed her somehow.

"Before I allow some of the other students to comment, I would like to make some suggestions of my own. I think it's important for me to have this input..." Sabine looks at me. "Oliver... as much as I like the story, I think you need to do more research on the subject of driving under the influence. It seems as though this situation is quite unlikely, in my opinion. As you know, stories must primarily be believable...and my view on the matter is that this story is not. While I'm aware that driving after smoking marijuana is against the law, I don't believe that being high can cause a car crash that's so catastrophic. After all, I'm sure we can all attest to the fact that smoking a joint doesn't make us lose our sense entirely."

The other students laugh, but I'm not laughing with them. I can feel rage boiling inside me like a volcano waiting to erupt. Not because I disagree with her, but because she has no idea what this story means to me. How can I be unaffected when the basis of it is true?

"The character herself is also difficult to connect with. We learn by the end that she was responsible for her husband's death…she was the one driving under the influence, after all. Perhaps if she was a drunk driver, it might be more believable…but if you want us to feel sorry for the character after it all becomes clear, then this isn't the way to write the story. If she was in the passenger seat and was the one who survived…do you see where I'm going with this, Oliver? It's not easy to sympathise with her the way things are right now."

I'm fully aware that my silence isn't helping me. I need to say something. The whole class is staring at me. Willow's eyes are full of sympathy and it's making me feel sick. I curl my hands into fists. Normally, I take criticism well. But today, I have to defend myself.

"Sabine… this piece is very personal to me. It's based on my own experience with the matter, and having you criticise it for being unrealistic…well I guess all I can say is that you're wrong. I don't need to research the subject because I've lived through it. And maybe you don't find the character likeable…maybe she doesn't have to be. I don't think I can ever look at the woman it's based on the same again…her actions ended a life."

The whole class falls silent. I hold my breath, feeling even more anxious than when I walked into the room. I can feel Willow's eyes on me as she tries to figure out something to say, but I don't want anyone to say anything. I can tell that Sabine is distressed, but I can't say I feel sorry for her. It feels as though she's bulldozed over my chest and now I can barely breathe. I opened up and this is what I get? To be told that my reality is unbelievable is laughable. This life isn't pretty, but it's the one I've got. Putting it down on paper made it feel even more real.

But I guess I should be glad that no one else understands. What happened between my mother and father in that car ended one life and ruined many others, mine included. These people who are looking at me like I'm crazy...they're the lucky ones. They're lucky to have the privilege of calling the piece of writing in front of them fiction and not realism.

I can't take this anymore. I don't want to be here. I have embarrassed myself in front of my peers and Sabine has made me feel about three inches tall. I mutter something about having a headache as I stand to leave the classroom, forgetting to pack my bag and heading for the door.

Blood is thumping in my ears as I storm away. Rumours travel fast. It won't be long until everyone is talking about my little breakdown in the seminar. My reputation is clearly on the line and the thought makes my heart flutter.

I burst into the men's bathroom and find it empty. As my chest tightens, I stumble into a cubicle and shut the door, sitting on the top of the toilet seat with my knees hugged to my chest. I haven't had a panic attack in a long time. I kind of thought I got all of that under control when I came to England. But maybe I just buried all these feelings under copious amounts of alcohol and fake smiles. Maybe I'll never heal from the incident that broke apart my family. And now that I've reopened old wounds, there's definitely no going back.

I guess that'll teach me not to make things personal…

Willow

I can't stop thinking about Oliver. After our seminar this morning, I should have known he wouldn't turn up to the afternoon lectures, but I've been looking out for him all the same. As our seminar came to an awkward close, I grabbed Oliver's things, planning to give them back to him in the afternoon lecture. But I can see now that his pride was hurt badly and he's not going to let that go easily. I guess it's safe to say that Oliver's facade has finally slipped.

And it's also safe to say that I've misjudged him. I never expected him to have such a raw and emotional past. As far as I can tell from his attitude, he's just a rich American boy used to getting what he wants. He certainly acts like he's got the whole world in the palm of his hand. But if his short story is anything to go by, it seems that his life is more complicated than he's ever let on.

Maybe I shouldn't be so judgemental. I pride myself on being an empath, and yet when it comes to him, I've always been determined to see the negatives. But it turns out that I was too quick to judge. After all, you never know what's going on in a person's life. Sure, every time I see him, he's smiling. Sure, he acts entitled and it's his least likeable quality. Sure, he makes me jealous of the things he has that I don't. But if someone close to him died in a car crash because the driver was high...who can blame him for trying to hide that from the world?

I'm hiding things too. I guess we're more alike than I thought. Now, all I want to do is let him know that he's not alone. I want to tell him things I've never told anyone. I want to let him know that things have never been easy for me either, so I know how he feels.

And yet we're not friends. We're barely even acquaintances. Guys like him only open up once in a while and when they get shot down, they realise the reason they never opened up in the first place is because it hurts too much. I should know. Sometimes it feels like it's easier to bear your own burdens than to share them with someone else. But I know one thing for sure. Being alone is even harder. And that's why I need to speak to him as soon as possible...to let him know he has someone.

Whether he wants my help or not, I have to try and help him. And that means trying to rebuild every bridge I've burned with him.

Now that classes are over for the day, I have to work a shift at the coffee shop. I lug my things - as well as Oliver's - over to the storeroom, all the while considering messaging Oliver. I guess he'll be wanting his things back, which would give me the perfect opportunity to talk to him, but I don't want him to think I'm being nosey. After all, the fact that we're not friends might make my concerns seem fleeting and fake. If I'm honest, of course I'm curious about what happened to him, but I have no plans to dig deeper if he's not interested in talking. I know if I were in his shoes, I'd want to forget the whole thing. I sigh as I prepare a latte for an impatient customer. I don't need this kind of new complication in my life. I've got enough on my plate. But Oliver opened up my eyes today. I can't shut him out again now.

I spend a while trying to figure out what I'm going to say to him. To my surprise, however, fifteen minutes into my shift, I see him walk in through the door. The distress that was so evident on his face earlier is gone, and I know that he's used the past few hours to get his head together. He's got a reputation to maintain, after all. There's no queue so he comes straight up to the counter, offering me the warmest smile I've ever received from him.

"Hey... how was the rest of class?"

I don't know how to play this. I can guarantee he doesn't want my sympathy, at least. I settle for raising my eyebrow.

"Dull in comparison, I must admit. It was certainly less dramatic."

To my relief, Oliver laughs at my poor attempt at a joke. At least he's still in good spirits. "Well, I'm sorry to disappoint, but I won't be coming back to that class…I've requested a change in tutor. I think Sabine and I have reached the end of the road."

"I know things didn't go well…but I don't think she meant to offend you."

Oliver sighs. "Yeah, I can see that now…but I feel uncomfortable going back there after the way I acted. I plan to speak to her about the whole thing, but I think it's best if we part ways."

I nod in understanding. In his shoes, I would do the exact same thing. Still, it's nice to see that he's been mature about this whole thing. He could easily throw Sabine under the bus, but maybe I misjudged the kind of guy he is if I think he would do that. Today is showing me a new side to Oliver, and it's piqued my curiosity to say the least.

"Well, it will be a shame not to see you in class anymore. Your stories always make me feel…well…"

Oliver leans against the counter with a wry smile that makes my stomach flutter.

"Go on... say what's on your mind."

"...hopeful? In the sense that when I read work by the other students, I feel as though I'm reading something written by a child. When I read something you've written... it's like delving into any good book. I wouldn't ever question that it's written by a *writer,* you know? And just for the record... I always find your work entirely believable."

Oliver's cheeks turn red. I've never seen him blush before and it makes the corners of my mouth upturn.

"Not what you were expecting?"

He chuckles. "To be honest, Willow, absolutely not. I've never thought of you as one of my biggest fans…"

"Don't flatter yourself. I like you as a writer, not necessarily as a person," I tell him, but my voice is soft. He smiles back and I know that he gets that I'm teasing him.

"Maybe you're finally going to give me a chance to change your mind."

I scoff. "Like you've been trying all this time?"

"I have, Willow. You just made up your mind about me a long time ago."

I find myself pulling at my hair, feeling nervous. *No one* makes me nervous. Not like this. I don't quite know where things shifted between us and yet there's…*something*. Something different. I try to keep my cool.

"The only conversations we ever have are about you liking my hair."

"That's called a compliment, Willow."

"I always assumed you were winding me up. Poking fun."

Oliver's face softened.

"If I ever gave you that impression then I'm truly sorry. I love your hair. It was one of the first things I noticed about you."

Now I'm really hot under the collar. I had no idea that Oliver Bachelor had ever truly noticed me. Despite my hair, despite the brash makeup and the tattoos, I've gotten pretty good at just fading into the background. I sometimes think about the fact that I'll leave university without and friends, without a legacy beyond my writing in the magazines. Maybe that's why it means so much to me to grab the top spot this year. So I don't leave here without making my mark at all. But now to hear that Oliver *noticed* me? It's pathetic how much I needed to hear that today.

And now he's looking at me with those green eyes of his and I feel too *seen*. It's been a long time since anyone looked at me like this. It makes me squirm a little. I clear my throat.

"Hey, I actually picked up your things from class...I can go get them for you."

"That would be great."

I leave my place behind the counter to go and find his bag. I hastily put all his papers in there earlier, so I feel a little bad that they're all crumpled, but he looks grateful as I hand it to him once I return. He glances inside his bag, looking for something in particular.

"Here… I didn't want to leave without giving you this." He hands me three pieces of paper covered in his messy scrawled handwriting. I quickly realise the paper contains the story I wrote for this week's class, and his annotations are written in just about every gap on the paper. I glance up at him and he smiles.

"I never got to give you your feedback…you've always been so helpful in the workshops. In fact, wherever I head next, I doubt the feedback I get will be as useful as yours…I didn't want to leave the seminar without giving you something in return."

I find that I'm blushing now. It's irrational, but I've always felt that I was at odds with Oliver in some way. We both want the same things, have the same goals, and I guess that puts us head to head. Now, as we're exchanging niceties, everything is changing. Why do I feel so much closer to him than I did this morning? Why do I feel like we've made an unspoken bond through two small acts of kindness? Why does it feel like I've misjudged him all along when nothing has really happened to change my mind?

"Thank you," I tell him quietly. "I really value your opinion, actually."

Oliver smirks. "Look at us getting along nicely. Makes a nice change, doesn't it? Seems that this is the start of something beautiful."

I smile involuntarily. He seems to have that effect on me now, whether I like it or not. As he's turning to walk away, I get this strange feeling that it's now or never. That if I want to be his friend, or even something more, I have to put myself forward now before he leaves and I don't get the chance.

"I want to join your writer's group," I blurt. Oliver turns back to look at me with a smile.

"I thought you'd never ask," he says as though he was certain I'd say it all along. That cockiness is back, but it doesn't seem quite so annoying now. "And as it turns out...our next meeting is tomorrow, right before my party. So I guess you'll have to attend both..."

I can feel anxiety stirring inside me. I have so much work to do...taking a whole night off for some party is out of the question. And yet part of me knows that I can't keep living like this. Spending all my time alone is no way to live. And now that Oliver and I have struck up something that I don't understand...I want to see how far we can take this.

I offer Oliver a smile.

"What time? I'll be there…"

CHAPTER THREE

Oliver

As days go, my Thursday was a mixed bag. I managed to lose my best tutor in the morning and humiliation was served for breakfast, but in the afternoon...well, Willow made it all better. After three years of asking, she's finally agreed to come to my writer's circle meeting.

I had to try my hardest to hide my shock when she said she wanted to join. After all, she's always seemed like a social recluse. I always took her refusal to join as a personal thing, but after our little bonding session...well, it made up for the morning's events, at least.

I still cringe thinking about how I walked out of the classroom. I still hate that I'm a talking point among my friends because of it. But knowing that I'll see Willow tonight...it makes me feel alive. I've enjoyed these years of winding her up - she gives as good as she gets, after all - but now, I'm looking forward to the next step in our relationship.

Getting along.

And now, my Friday is going to be great. I can feel it in my bones. I've been up since seven and I've made a fry up for Violet and I to eat before we study. She's been lounging in my bedroom, but as the smell of eggs and bacon wafts through the apartment, she pops her head around the corner.

She's wearing an oversized tee and nothing else, but since my night thinking about Willow, I haven't been able to look at Violet the same. After all, she's my best friend. The benefits between us don't make me feel romantically toward her. All of a sudden, it's hard to imagine why we ever started sleeping together in the first place.

"Smells good," she comments.

"At least something does. Get a shower," I tease, gesturing at her messy bed-head. She stayed over last night to distract me from the day I'd had, but Willow being on my mind was enough to keep me occupied anyway. For the first time in a while, sleeping in the same bed together became innocent and nothing happened between us.

Violet pouts at me, running a hand through her hair. "What? Suddenly you don't think I look cute in the mornings?"

I laugh as I serve up our food. "When have I ever said that you do?"

Violet doesn't respond, sitting down at the table and accepting a plate from me. As I tuck right in, though, she holds off, watching me intently. I pause with my fork close to my mouth.

"Take a picture...it lasts longer."

She offers me a sad smile, reaching out to ruffle my hair. "I might just do that...hey, I was thinking…"

"Don't overexert yourself…"

Violet rolls her eyes, and I can tell she's not in the mood for my teasing right now. "Let's leave coursework until another day...it's been a while since we did anything fun!"

"We were literally out drinking a few days ago...plus writer's circle...plus we hung out last night and watched a movie…"

"Right...but I thought maybe we could go somewhere. Like, you've been in Liverpool for three years now and you still haven't been to the Beatles museum…"

"Come on, Vi. You know that I think the Beatles are kind of overrated...especially considering this city produced Echo and the Bunnymen."

"Okay sure...but we could do something else. Just the two of us."

I look up at her with an amused smile. She looks so serious right now, as though we don't spend every waking hour in each other's presence. I dig into my food.

"Look, I hear you. It's nice outside...I'd like to do something fun. But let's get real. Tonight we're going to get super drunk which means tomorrow will be a write off. After my seminar yesterday I've got to tread carefully...I've got a new tutor to impress and my attendance record stinks. Let's study today and chill tomorrow, yeah? We can go to the museum or whatever. Though I don't know why you're so keen on that all of a sudden...we've never done that before."

Violet shrugs, avoiding my eyes. "Yeah, I know...I thought that's why we should do it."

"Okay, so we will. Tomorrow. You can show me what all the Beatles fuss is about, right?"

Violet nods, pushing her beans around her plate. She's usually got a good appetite, so I can tell something's up. I nudge her with my knee under the table.

"Hey...I know coursework sucks, but I just want to keep on top of it."

Violet raises an eyebrow. "That's never been a concern of yours before."

"What can I say...I'm a changed man." I sigh. "It's just...I was talking to Willow the other day, and she made me realize...well, I've got to start taking things more seriously."

"Willow? Who is Willow?"

I frown. "You know her, Violet. She's in our lectures. She serves us coffee twice a week. Vibrant blue hair, cute smile, curvy...."

"Oh...yeah. Why were you talking to her?"

"What, so I'm not allowed to talk to other people?" I laugh, shaking my head. "She's kind of cool. I guess I've overlooked her a little in the past. She's always around, but we never spend any time together...but she's got a lot about her, you know? She's one of the best writers I've met since moving here. She's quirky, she's funny without even trying, she's not a suck up...I get the feeling she doesn't care what people think. Like, either they like her or they don't, but she won't change for anyone. She makes me feel...excited, I guess? Like, I feel a bit nervous around her, but in a good way."

"I didn't realize I asked for her life story," Violet says with an aloof sniff. "Sounds like someone's got a crush."

I can't help smiling a little. "Yeah…maybe I do."

The whole room falls silent. It almost gives me a chill. Violet puts down her knife and fork and stands up abruptly, not looking at me.

"You know what? I think I'll grab a shower and head home."

"But I thought we were going to study today? And then we've got the writer's circle…"

"I'll just come back later. I might go out and do something. And I know you're busy, so…"

"Well, maybe the girls are free? I heard Abby mention something about brunch on Bold Street…"

"I'll figure it out. Later."

Violet leaves the room without saying another word and I feel myself deflate in the chair. The atmosphere between us turned pretty cold the second I mentioned Willow. I don't know what her problem is. Does she think Willow is beneath her? Or does she find it hard to understand Willow's sarcastic demeanor and think she's a bitch? She's never expressed any feelings toward her in either direction…and of course, she just pretended not to know her, even though I've heard her mention Willow before. So is there something going on that I'm missing? Or am I imagining that Violet suddenly went cold?

I guess I'll find out tonight at the writer's circle meeting.

Willow

For the first time in a while, I feel excited for the evening ahead. For once, I won't be stuck at home working and listening to my noisy neighbors having fun around me. I'm even taking the opportunity to walk through town, meandering through Bold Street on a detour to Oliver's apartment. I know that I shouldn't be doing this, but I deserve this break, and I'm sure as hell not going to waste it.

I should be nervous, I guess. I've never really hung out with my peers before. Even back when we were in first year and we were constantly encouraged to join societies or attend mixers, I was forced to keep to myself because I was working. Now, for the first time in three years, I'm making an effort. But I feel like I know these people well enough to have a good time tonight. I've got a cheap bottle of rose wine, my favorite yellow pants and black off-shoulder top on, and I'm feeling cute. Plus, seeing Oliver tonight feels like it's going to be a bonus.

Who am I kidding…he's the reason I want to come at all. He's been on my mind constantly these last few days. Having a crush this potent is both embarrassing and inconvenient, and yet it's nice to feel *something* other than stress. It's been a long time since I had any sort of attachment to anyone.

Maybe I can indulge a little, even if he's obviously not feeling the same way about me.

I approach his flat with butterflies in my stomach, but they're completely the good kind. I've never been nervous to mingle, I've just been in need of time. I guess tonight really has to go well for me to make some connections, but I'm quietly confident. At least I'll come away from tonight feeling a little closer to Oliver.

I ring for his flat and he buzzes me in, so I navigate the corridors alone, following the sounds of chatter down the hallway. It's posh in here, much nicer than the normal halls of residence that students tend to be in. It's worlds away from my grotty flat even though it's only a ten minute walk from here. It makes me ache for what I could've had, but I push those thoughts aside. Tonight is supposed to be fun, and I intend to make it that way.

I balance my wine in the crook of my elbow and awkwardly open the door. As I walk in, I see familiar faces all around. Some people are sitting down, but at least ten people are standing up just chatting. This writer's circle is much bigger than I expected. And as I close the door, everyone looks around to see who I am.

They don't look impressed.

I offer a smile, trying not to show my nerves, but everyone here looks at me as though I'm a total stranger. Their eyes are far from friendly. And then I catch Violet's eye from across the room. She looks so effortlessly cool with her sharp bob and her tiny body shrouded in an oversized jumper. She's nursing a glass of red wine and pursing her lips at me as though someone brought me in on the bottom of their shoe. No one makes an effort to greet me at all. Though plenty of people have simply carried on their conversations, it feels like the room has fallen silent.

"Hi…" I say, awkwardly waving in the general direction of the group. "Nice to see you all…"

I'm completely relieved when after a few agonizing seconds, Oliver pops his head around the corner. He's got a jug of water in one hand and a glass of gin in the other. He turns to see me and grins. Violet's eyes bore into mine for a final second before she turns her back on us completely.

"Willow, you came!" Oliver says, putting down the jug and walking over to greet me with an unexpected hug. I almost drop my wine and I'm too surprised to hug him back, but the warmth of his body and the smell of his earthy cologne is enough to make me feel at home. I feel a strange tug toward him, an unexpected sexual lurch in my stomach that makes me want to do something stupid like kiss him in front of everyone. When he pulls away, I'm red faced, embarrassed by my sudden rush of feelings for him as though everyone here knows what I'm thinking. He's smiling and it makes me feel as though he's actually happy to see me. Like he's just been waiting for me to get here.

"We were just about to start the writer's circle, actually...come and sit with me since it's your first time. You're not nervous, are you?"

The corners of my lips twitch.

"Nah," I say, though the cold welcome from the group has made me a little uncertain. I tell myself that I was imagining it. These people are my classmates. They'll make an effort, I'm sure of it.

"Good. Let's sit down…"

He grabs my wrist to lead me away and my skin tingles at his touch. I can't remember ever touching him before tonight, but it feels so good to have his skin on mine. I've never had good enough friends to be much of a hugger or a toucher, but with his fingers curled around my wrist, I can see the appeal. I wonder if he can feel my heartbeat pulsing against his hand. I wonder if he'll understand that it's him that's making my heart race a little faster. I wonder if he'll take a hint and thread his fingers through mine…

He doesn't, but the room is cramped as people fight for places to sit, and even though he eventually gets us seated on the floor, I don't mind one bit. I cross my legs, glad to be wearing trousers, and our knees brush against one another. I hold my breath, but he doesn't move an inch. Our legs remain pressed together.

"Does everyone have a drink?" Oliver addresses the room, grinning all the while. It's easy now to see how easily likeable he is. When he's in a room full of people who adore him, I can see that his friendly exterior isn't as insincere as it comes across. He's full of that American charm that has surpassed us Brits entirely, leaving us with a deadly combination of sarcasm and passive-aggressiveness. But then again, I suppose over there, they see us all as overly polite tea drinkers who love the monarchy and Oasis…

Everyone settles themselves and looks at Oliver for further instruction. I can feel eyes lingering on me, and I wonder why Violet isn't sitting with Oliver. She glares at me from afar and I duck my head. I'm not interested in confrontation tonight. I just want things to go well.

"Thanks for coming, everyone! You know how much I love these nights…and since we're all drinking something or other, let's count this as pre-drinks…"

Several of the boys cheer and everyone laughs, including me. It feels good to be a part of something, even if I still feel like I'm on the fringe of it all.

"Before we get started…we have a new writer with us tonight. I know Willow hasn't been to many of the social events since we started, so I thought I'd start us off with reading some of her writing. I passed you guys her short story that she wrote for a seminar this week as you came in through the door…so while we all enjoy a nice drink, we can read it over and then maybe give some feedback? Let's chill out, people. It's Friday…best night of the week to get our creative juices flowing."

Everyone murmurs in agreement and I can't help blushing. I can't believe he's brought my story for everyone to read. When I look his way he leans in to whisper to me as everyone begins their contemplative reading.

"I thought everyone deserved to be blessed with brilliance tonight," he murmurs.

I chuckle. "How long have you been sitting on that compliment?"

"Oh, only for three years...since I first read your stories."

I'm blushing again. Is this flirting? In the case of a writer, there's no higher compliment than someone praising your work. But this feels personal too...like he's praising me as well. I watch as his eyes drag over my body and I feel the scorch of his gaze on my skin. He sees that I'm watching him and he gives me a slow, sultry smile before turning his face to the paper in his hand to read the story. Without him watching me so intently, it's easier to breathe, giving me time to recover from the way he looked at me. Soon enough, though, I'm wishing he'd look at me again.

I sit sipping my wine from a plastic party cup and watch the rest of the room get lost in my story. The harsh faces I saw around the room before seem to soften, as though my writing has changed their opinions of me. But when I look at Violet, she hasn't even bothered to look at my writing. She's chugging wine like it's no one's business and scowling to herself. I rake through my memories, trying to recall if I've done anything to upset her over the years. Maybe she's just in a bad mood tonight...it's none of my business, really. But I can't get over the nagging feeling that I've done something to upset her. Unless she can somehow read my thoughts about Oliver, then she has no reason to hate me, surely?

"Alright!" Oliver says as people begin to finish the story. "Let's give people a little longer to finish up...but for those who have already finished, have a chat with someone in the room and see what they think!"

Several people begin chatting and I rise to my feet, moving toward Violet before I can stop myself. I don't know why I feel the need to go over there. I'd be much more comfortable sitting beside Oliver and chatting like before. But by the time I come to a halt next to her and she looks up at me, I realize there's no going back.

"I didn't read the story," she says coldly. I sip my wine and force a smile.

"That's okay. I wasn't expecting my story to be on the agenda tonight anyway...I just came to mingle a little," I reply. She folds her arms.

"Why have you come up out of the woodwork all of a sudden?" she asks me. There's no getting around the fact that she's being rude to me. There's no other way to interpret what she's saying. I find myself stepping back defensively which is entirely unlike me.

"I have a night off for once...I usually work evenings."

Violet raises her eyebrows. "Right. Well most people don't just show up after three years and try to wriggle their way in. It's kind of rude, you know."

I blink several times. I don't know how I thought this conversation would go, but it certainly wasn't like this. It's clear to me now that she doesn't like me. Maybe she finds something about me offensive...I've heard it all before. Girls like me get a lot of stick. I'm plus-sized, blue-haired and plain speaking. Girls like Violet seem to hate those things about me because they're narrow-minded. I'm speculating, but one graze of her eyes over me tells me she doesn't like what she sees, for whatever reason. I pity her, in a way. It's like she wants me to tick a bunch of boxes in order to be likeable; skinny, pretty, quiet. I'll never be those things and that's fine by me. I can only imagine why it matters to her. I look at her and see a beautiful woman with insecurities inbuilt. She's nothing like me, which is fine. But she's determined to hate the differences between us...and perhaps that's why we'll never get along.

"Sorry if you find it rude. That wasn't my intention," I tell her, managing to uphold my smile. "I'd love to hang out with you guys more...it's just hard since I have two jobs. My loan doesn't cover my rent…"

"So you're basically saying you're too busy for us," Violet says with a sniff. She raises her glass to her lips and takes a long sip, knowing I'm stumped as to what to say. When she swallows, her lips purse once again. "Don't force yourself, Willow. We'll all be fine without you here."

I wasn't expecting the comment to hurt so much, but somehow, it does. I've never had someone act so bitterly toward me for no reason. Other than my father, that is. I can see hatred in her eyes as she stares me down. She's waiting for a reaction from me and she might be about to get one. Tears sting my eyes and I hide my emotions by taking a sip of wine.

"Alright," I say eventually, too wounded to come up with a quick response. "I'll leave you to it."

I return to Oliver's side, feeling like a child hiding behind their mother's legs. In only a matter of minutes, Violet has taken my mood from high to lower than low. I can't help looking around the room now and wondering if everyone here feels the same way as she does. No one is paying me much mind - why would they when they're surrounded by their friends? - but do they despise me being here? Are they secretly wishing they weren't stuck here, reading my writing, breathing my air? Violet certainly seems to feel that way. In fact, the second I sit down, I watch as she disappears from the room entirely, as though she can't even bear to be in the room with me anymore.

"Alright, Willow?" Oliver asks me, his cheery smile stuck in place. "What were you and Vi talking about?"

I could tell him. I could tell him that his girlfriend has a problem with me and then he might ask me to leave. But I have as much right to be here as anyone else. I was invited by the host. He's been asking me to come for years, so what's wrong with me accepting the invitation? I roll my shoulders back and swallow back my tears. I can't allow her to get to me.

"Nothing," I tell him, "Nothing at all."

CHAPTER FOUR

Oliver

The party is in full swing now, and I haven't seen Willow in some time. I saw her chatting to a few people from our screenwriting class earlier, but now, she's not visible in my living room or kitchen area. I don't think she'd go home without telling me...so where is she?

I've been distracted since she arrived. I've felt the need to talk to her all night and yet, the first opportunity I've had to pin her down, she's somewhere where I can't find her. As soon as the writer's circle meeting finished, she went to top up her wine and she's been out of my reach ever since.

I want to get her alone. I want somewhere to talk where it's just me and her. For once, the hustle and bustle of a great party can't entice me. Everyone here is having a good time, except me. I'm standing with Violet and our other friends, half listening to their conversation about Sabine's class while I keep an eye out for Willow.

"What's wrong with you?" Violet hisses as she nudges my elbow. "It's like you're not even here."

"Sorry...I'm just distracted."

"You're not drunk enough," our friend Hugo says, his scraggly hair covering up the glazed over look in his eyes. He's probably drunk enough for the both of us. "Have another beer. Hey, where's your friend? The newbie?"

"Willow?" I ask, brightening a little. "Hey, wasn't her story great? She's so talented. Everyone in our seminar group is obsessed with her work."

Hugo snorts. "Are you serious? You're getting hyped over her? Dude, she's completely lame."

I blink several times. "What? You think so?"

"Ugh, please," Alice butts in, rolling her eyes as Hugo swings an arm around her shoulders. "She just came here to show off. Obviously she's good at writing...big deal. Like, she literally just wanted to sit here and listen to us all praising her."

"That's not true...she didn't even know we'd be reading her work tonight. She's just trying to be friendly."

"Face it, Oliver, she's a snob," Violet says sourly. "She acts like she's too good for the rest of us. The way she always lords over us because she has a job at the cafe and we're all just focussing on our studies...like she's so much better than us just because she has a part time job. It's so irritating. I don't know why you like her at all."

I scowl. "Now hold on a minute...she's not like that at all. She has a good work ethic, sure, but-"

"Hey, didn't she have a go at you the other day for not turning up to class?" Violet points out, taking a smug sip of her wine. Alice groans.

"Oh God, she's the worst. Such a suck-up. It's no wonder she gets such good grades. I bet she's tight with all the tutors…"

"Probably shagging half of them," Hugo grins.

"Don't be a dick, Hugo," I snap. He always takes jokes too far, but he doesn't seem to care.

Alice gives me a patronizing smile. "Look, it's no big deal, Oliver. Just don't ask her here again, yeah? She doesn't fit in."

"You guys haven't even given her a chance!" I say, raising my voice a little louder than I should, but I can't help it. This conversation is driving me mad. "She's been nothing but lovely all evening. Hugo, she was really helpful with feedback for your poetry…"

"Are you kidding? She thinks she knows better than me…her poetry sucks," Hugo scowls. "She had nothing good to say about it."

"You're twisting everything…"

Violet rolls her eyes. "Get a grip. You can't force us to like her. She's never going to be one of us. Just let it go."

I turn on my heel and walk away. Hugo's laughter rings in my ears as I push past my classmates. I can feel anger boiling in my blood. I don't know what's happening to me lately. I've heard them joking about Willow in the past. Just the occasional comment here and there that I've never agreed with, but never argued with either. And now, it makes me so angry to hear them talking about her that way. I need to get out of here. I need to talk to someone sane.

There's a balcony adjoining my living area that overlooks the city. There are a few smokers out there, but they disperse when they see me heading out. I close the sliding door behind me and dial my sister's number. She'll talk some sense into me.

She picks up after several rings. "Thank God you called. I'm bored out of my mind over here. It's late where you are...are you having a party?"

I breathe in the cool air, trying to calm myself down. "Yeah."

"Well what are you ringing me for, then? You need something? Or are you going to drunkenly tell me how much I mean to you?"

"Tammy, listen...I need some advice."

"Alright, straight to the chase then."

"It's about a girl."

Tammy falls silent for a moment and then she laughs. "Oh man, you took me by surprise then...you want to talk about girls? What makes you think I can help?"

"Well...you are one? And you've dated more girls than I have."

"You're the one in a long-standing casual relationship with your best friend…"

"Is that what you'd call it?"

"Well it depends whose perspective you look at it from...from where she's standing, she probably thinks you guys are a thing. I mean, she's probably expecting that you're official, even if you haven't confirmed it."

I scrunch my eyes closed, running a hand through my hair. "Well...then I might have made a mistake."

"Go on."

I sigh, leaning against the balcony barrier. "I've found someone I like. And she's great. Which I keep telling Violet...and now it makes sense why she hates this girl so much."

"Oh, Oliver...I thought you were meant to be the smooth one in this family? Don't you understand girls at all?"

"I don't need a lecture, Tammy, I already know I've screwed up...I need you to tell me what to do."

Tammy sighs. "Tell me about the girl. The one you like."

"Willow? Well...she's gorgeous. And so cool...she's got blue hair and a great sense of style...she's a hard-worker and she always says things as they are...she's fearless. And one of the best writers I've met here."

Tammy sighs dreamily. "Sounds like you really admire her. Look, I know Violet is your best friend...but I've been waiting a long time to hear you say that you're into someone. Like, for real, and not just that you think someone's cute or you want to have sex with them."

"Have I ever really been like that?"

"Man, you were a menace before you went over to England, trust me. Anyway...I know you don't get feelings. Or at least not that you've admitted before. So you've got to go for it. And end things with Violet...like, ASAP. She's only going to get her heart broken. And that means being discreet too...if Willow likes you back, that is."

"So...who do I talk to first?"

"I guess it depends on whether this girl likes you back...just don't do anything stupid or rash, okay? Think this through...you've got a big heart, but you're not always the most sensitive soul. You care about them both, but Violet's your best friend. You have to make sure not to damage her heart. Because from what you've told me she's kind of mean sometimes...but it's because she's protective of you. She wants you for herself, Olly...and she can't have you. You need to make that clear."

I sigh. Tammy's right. She always is. "Alright...I'll do that. I'll speak to both of them. Thanks, Tammy...I owe you one."

"Hey, it's fine...when you come back over to the US, you can make it up to me by getting me out of the house once in a while. I'm going crazy over here."

"I know." I pause. "I miss you, Tammy."

I hear her breath catch in her throat. But then she laughs. "Alright, you're entering soppy territory now. Go find Willow. And don't mess it up."

I chuckle quietly. "I'll do my best. Thank you, Tammy."

"Don't sweat it. Hey, have a beer for me. And let me know how it goes."

She hangs up before I can and I sigh. There's still things I want to say to Tammy. I want to let her know that she's not alone out in America with Mom. I'll always be there for her when she needs me. But she's right. I need to fix the mess I've made on this side of the pond. Tomorrow, I'll call her and talk properly.

But right now, I want to speak to Willow.

I head back inside and there's still no sign of her. Unless she went home, there's only one other place she can be. I push through the crowds, hoping not to see Violet on my way. I manage to make it to my bedroom. There's a light on in the room so I assume it's safe to enter. I slip into the room as quietly as I can.

I catch sight of her right away. She's sitting on my bed with her back to me. I lean against the door with a smile. I must be in deep if just seeing the back of her head can make me smile so much.

"Hey. What're you doing sneaking in my room? You're supposed to wait for an invite," I say jokingly. Willow turns to look at me and my face falls. Her eyes are filled with tears.

"I'm sorry...I didn't mean to be rude...I just wanted a bit of privacy."

I walk slowly to sit next to her, not wanting to spook her. I want to put my arm around her, but the gesture seems forbidden somehow.

"Hey, I was just kidding...what's up? Did something happen?"

Willow throws her hands up in exasperation. I can tell she's irritated at herself for crying, but tears still trickle down her cheeks. "Everything was fine...and then I overheard someone saying that I shouldn't have been invited...that I don't belong here...that I was a pity invite. God, I don't normally let things like that get to me, but...well, it's not the first time I've heard someone say those things tonight."

"Willow...you know that's not true, right?"

Willow glances at me, wiping her face. "It's not?"

"It's definitely not. I've wanted you here all along, Willow...I thought you knew that."

She shrugs. "Well...it just seems like you might be the only person who feels that way."

"You can never please everyone…"

"You can. You do."

I laugh. "Trust me, I've pissed a few people off in my time. And Violet...well, she's pissed at me right now."

"Why?"

"I'm not here to talk about her...I want to know you're okay."

Willow sighs and wipes her eyes. "I'm fine. I'm a big girl, I can handle it. But I think I'll go home...coming here was a mistake."

"Willow...stay a while. We can sit here...just you and me."

Willow looks at me with her big sad eyes. "Why?"

"Because I want to."

"But why? I'm completely unapproachable to everyone else at this party...what makes you want to stay here with me?"

I can't help myself. One look at her lips and I know what I want more than anything in the world.

I lean in and kiss her.

Willow

His lips taste like strawberry gin. They're warm and inviting. I can barely believe he's kissing me, but I close my eyes and allow it to happen.

I want it to happen.

His hand slides to my waist and he pulls me in closer to him. It feels like a long time since someone actually touched me. There's electricity dancing on my skin. I cup his cheek and feel his stubble brush against my hand. Everything I'm feeling seems so new and exciting and I never want it to end.

But then I remember Violet.

I pull away harshly and stand up. Oliver looks completely confused. I'll bet he's not used to women yanking away from him mid-kiss. But I can't do this. I can't be the reason their relationship turns to tatters. And more importantly, I don't want to be Oliver's escapism project from Violet. I want him to want me...not just because I'm here and vulnerable and more available than his girlfriend.

"Willow?"

I don't look back as I head out of the bedroom and shove my way through my classmates. I hear them sniggering as I leave, but I know now that none of them are worth my time. Not one of them. None of them wanted me there in the first place. Not even Oliver. Yes, I see it now. I was a pitiable distraction from the girl he loves. A way to make her jealous. That's why he picked my story. That's why he gave me special treatment all night. That's why he was so damn interested in what Violet and I were talking about, and the reason he was reluctant to say why she was angry at him.

I'm such a fool.

I can still taste him on my lips. I can still feel the tingle on my spine. I know it was childish of me to walk out of there without an explanation, but it was childish of him to drag me into his relationship issues. We're both idiots. But I won't fall for it again.

Once again, tears fill my eyes and I laugh at myself, wiping them away as I storm down the street. The evening was a nightmare from start to finish. I thought it would be worth it for him. But he's just like the rest of them.

So why am I aching to be with him right now?

I feel lonelier now than I have in a long time. I thought I was finally getting somewhere. I thought I'd found someone to relate to, someone with a softer side to them than appears on the surface...someone like me. Oliver could've been someone special in my life, even if he'd never decided to kiss me. I could've used a friend. And now I know that I can't trust him. Because any man that goes behind his woman's back is a man to be avoided. He was probably just messing around, seeing how far he could make me fall for him. But whatever his game is, he's the one person who'll come away unscathed.

I reach my flat. There are people smoking on the stairs beneath the beat up fire alarm. I'm firmly back in my own world, but even this is preferable to Oliver's fancy flat right now. I let myself into my flat and tell myself I'm lucky. Lucky that I don't have to rely on anyone else. Lucky to have a place of my own to keep away from the cruelty of the world. But with my door shut and the windows shut, the flat is horribly quiet for once. A reminder of how alone I am.

I want to be angry at him, and yet I'm not. I'm angry at myself. Angry for letting myself get my hopes up. Furious at my own naivety. I hate that I crave him. I crave the life he has, even though being a part of it tonight was awful. All it did was introduce me to rich people with a lifestyle of partying and bitching about one another. Maybe that's all money has to offer our world...it creates a bunch of people who think they can treat others like dirt just because they can pay their way to the top.

But I thought despite his money, he was different. I saw other things in him...his humour, his talent, his likability...his flirtatiousness. I curl up in a ball, feeling sorry for myself.

My phone buzzes on my desk. Part of me is hoping it's a message from Oliver, but it's not. It's some guy on a dating app asking me out for dinner tomorrow. It's his opening line. We haven't even had a conversation yet. Looking at his photographs, I'm not even sure why I swiped for him. But before I know what I'm doing, I'm replying to him to make plans. I don't see why I shouldn't. If he sucks, then it won't be any worse than tonight was. Maybe I'll get to know the guy and really like him.

Maybe it'll be a quick fix for getting over Oliver Bachelor.

CHAPTER FIVE

Oliver

I wake with the worst hangover in the world and a sense that something is very wrong. When I turn over, I find Violet lying in bed next to me, wearing nothing, but one of my t-shirts. My conversation with Tammy comes flooding back...and then my kiss with Willow.

Willow...I'm still trying to figure that girl out. I know I picked a bad time to kiss her. I really did. She was vulnerable and upset and I should've waited. But I still don't know why she got up and left. I tried to call her, but there was no response. And now I've got Violet in my bed and I have no recollection of what we said to each other.

This is a mess. I get up out of bed slowly, praying that the world will stop spinning, but I guess it's a punishment for my behaviour. I should've done things in a better way. I should've sat Violet down and explained to her that I don't want to continue our sexual relationship. I should've spent some more time getting to know Willow before diving on her like that. But I barely ever let logic stand in the way of my emotions. I'm used to acting on impulse. Now, for the first time, I'm truly seeing the results of that.

I stumble into my kitchen to make myself a coffee. There's mess everywhere; beer cans strewn on the floor, the remains of a Chinese takeout meal in my sink, and a pile of smashed glass in the corner of the room. I vaguely remember sweeping it up now, but not much else. After Willow left, I hit the drink pretty hard. Not one of my finer decisions.

And now I have to face up to everything. I have to tell Violet that I'm done, even after sharing a bed with her last night. I have to try and get to the bottom of what happened with Willow. And last of all, I have to do it all with a horrific hangover.

I wish my sister was here to talk this over with. Or better still, I wish Willow was here so we could talk. I'd go over to her place, but I don't know where she lives. Plus, if she's ignoring my calls, I'm sure she's got a good reason for doing so. No, I need to deal with one mess at a time. As much as I'd love to smooth things over with Willow, I have other things to worry about.

Before I can give it too much thought, I message my Bachelor Brother's chat. My siblings are the first people I always turn to for advice, even though they're scattered across the globe and completely out of reach.

I might be shouting into the void here...but I've got a problem. I kissed a girl I like last night, Willow...and she left straight after. I think I've upset her somehow...but I don't know how. And this morning, I woke up with Violet...I'm trying to break things off with her and...well, it's not going well. Advice is much needed.

It's bad timing; it's 2am in California so Tammy will be asleep, and she's the one who usually offers up the most sensible advice. But when I see that Ezra's replying to my message, I feel relieved.

Hey bro...sounds like a dilemma you've got yourself into. But give Willow some time and space...she'll come around. I wish I'd done that with Leo...pestering gets you nowhere. Women need to be able to breathe when they're angry and upset.

Says who? Tammy says, joining in the conversation. *If it were me, I'd want you to keep trying. A little effort goes a long way.*

You're up late, little sister, Caleb says.
Sorry, Mom.
*Well, I happen to agree with Ezra. If you leave her to her own devices, she'll come back to you. You've probably rubbed her up the wrong way…*Caleb adds wisely.
By kissing her?
Hey…maybe you did it wrong?
Very funny, Tammy.
Don't listen to her, bro. We've got your back, Caleb adds.
Spoken by two single men, Oliver. May I remind you that as the only woman in this chat, I have insider knowledge on the matter. I know what it's like to get in an argument with a man and to receive radio silence…it sucks. So if you don't want to lose her forever, you'll find a way to speak to her.

I can't argue with that. As usual, Tammy's come to the rescue.

Now, considering I'm sure you're hungover, get yourself some bacon and eggs, a glass of OJ and prepare yourself to talk to Violet. You have to call it off. Today.
I will. Thanks guys. I feel much better.

I tidy up the flat while my siblings continue chatting among themselves. The boys appear to be ganging up on Tammy for staying out after midnight with her friends, but hard as it is, I have to remind myself that she's eighteen now. Our youngest sibling is all grown up. And actually, when it comes to emotions, she's the smartest of us all. No doubt she'll be checking up on me later to see if I follow through with my plans to talk to Violet, but she doesn't need to worry. I'm going to cut right to the chase the second I see her.

She emerges just after I finish my breakfast. She looks good, even with her tousled hair and my baggy t-shirt hanging off her body. She seems much happier than she did last night as she leans against the doorway.

"You didn't make me any?"

"Not today…Violet, I want to talk."

Her smile slips a little. I think she knows what I want to say, but she's not going to make it easy for me to get the words out. I'm about to speak, to just blurt it all out, but she interrupts me.

"Well, we're not doing anything today…let's go out for dinner. We can talk then."

"Violet, come on…don't drag this out."

"Drag what out?" she asks innocently. "What, I'm not allowed to ask you out for dinner anymore?"

"We've never done that…"

"So let's change that. Liverpool has loads of great food places. We barely ever eat out."

"Vi…"

"I'll make a reservation, shall I? I'll pick somewhere cool, I swear…"

"Violet!"

She leaves the room before I can speak again and I groan in frustration. She won't let me get a word in edgeways. But maybe it's better if we speak in public. That way, if she's angry at me, she can't cause a scene. Besides, it might be okay. Maybe Tammy was wrong. Maybe she doesn't care about me, at least not in that way. After all, we made an agreement to call things off if feelings ever got involved. I'm the one who wants to end it, not her…surely she would've said something by now if she was secretly crushing on me?

At least that's what I tell myself.

It's nearly seven o'clock when I show up for my reservation at an Indian restaurant with Violet. She's clearly made an effort for the occasion, her slim figure hugged by a short black dress. She's even wearing heels and it puts us at equal height. It's unlike Violet to dress up so much, so I wonder if she's sensed that there's a lot riding on this dinner. I just hope she doesn't think this is a date.

We get seated at a table and we're handed some menus, but I'm too anxious to look properly. I keep glancing up at Violet, who seems far too calm for my liking. She's smiling as she looks at her options and I suddenly get the sense that this was a terrible idea. I should've forced out the truth when we were back at the flat, even if it upset her. But now we're here I'm just going to have to make the best of it.

We order and Violet immediately leans in, looking pleased. Our knees nudge underneath the table.

"I can't remember the last time we did something like this…"

I shift uncomfortably. "We hang out a lot, Violet…it's nice to eat out for once, but it's not really a habit we should get into…"

Violet shrugs dreamily. "Let's just enjoy it for tonight, okay? You, me, good food, good conversation…I'm not asking too much, am I?"

My heart seizes. She looks so happy right now. How am I supposed to tell her that I don't want to continue the way we're going?

I never expected this to be so complicated. I've been naive to think she sees this the way I do. And now, we're in a pickle because of it.

"Violet…we need to discuss something."

She doesn't seem to sense my tone and continues smiling brightly. "What is it?"

I'm about to open my mouth to speak when I see something that makes my heart drop to my stomach. Or rather, someone. I can do nothing but stare until the moment her eyes meet mine.

Willow…

Willow

Oliver…what the hell is he doing here?

I can see him looking back at me, his eyes wide. Perhaps he didn't expect me to catch him here. It's not like we often bump into one another in public. But now the stars have clearly aligned to prove to me that I shouldn't be waiting on Oliver Bachelor. Obviously he's on a date with Violet. *Obviously* that kiss the other night meant nothing to him and everything to me. Obviously being out on a date with someone else was the right decision…

"Are you listening to me?"

I blink twice and my date comes back into focus. The man sitting opposite me is all kinds of attractive…at least to look at. He's got a strong jaw, curls to die for and piercing blue eyes that had me captivated for a split second when I first saw him.

But of course, he has the personality of a wet flannel. And now that I can see Oliver staring at me from across the room, his mouth gaping in surprise, I can't even remember my date's name.

"What are you staring at?" he asks, turning in his seat to see what's captured my attention. "Are you looking at some other guy?"

"No, no…I know him, we go to uni together," I say hastily. I can feel my cheeks heating up at this whole ordeal. "I'm sorry I didn't mean to be rude…tell me more about…um…your sports science degree."

He doesn't need to be told twice. Mr. Boring continues to talk as I try my hardest not to look in

Oliver's direction. Our food arrives, but I'm suddenly not hungry. As my date continues to talk, I feel anger rising inside me. Why is it that Oliver seems to turn up wherever I am? Why is it that he had to come here and flaunt his relationship with Violet to the world? Especially after the kiss we shared…

I can't think about that right now. I'm supposed to be in the moment. This was meant to be an enjoyable night off. I was hoping to end the night with some meaningless sex and then delete this guy from my dating app. I'm not searching for the one. And yet, one particular person just keeps appearing, as though reminding me of some destiny I never wanted. If he's my fate, my future, the one I'm meant to be with, then this isn't going the way I imagined love to manifest itself.

"Sorry, I feel like I've been hogging the limelight," my date tells me with a laugh. I think I've been zoned out of his talking for at least fifteen minutes, trying not to look in Oliver's direction. "Tell me more about you…"

I consider myself at least a mildly interesting person, but for once, there's not a thing I want to say about myself. I don't want to sell myself to this guy with funny stories about my past or a list of my achievements. At the end of the day, I couldn't care less about what he thinks of me. The only person I want to share that kind of information with is sitting in this room, breathing my air, but seemingly a million miles away. He already has someone to talk about these things with. The last thing he needs is me complicating things further.

"I just need to nip to the bathroom," I tell my date, and he's already returned to his food in seconds. He won't miss me when I go. I grab my bag and walk off towards the toilets, half tempted to try and leave. I don't want to be here. I don't care about how this date goes, but I care about being forced to watch Oliver so happy with Violet.

I hate the way he's captured my attention all of a sudden. I've always been able to suppress my feelings for someone if I know they're not interested, but I guess I feel a spark of hope with Oliver, even if I shouldn't. Or maybe it's just that I care more this time if things don't go right. Even if my heart gets messed around, I'll still have to see his face every day and know that I'm not good enough for him. I'll still have to accept that he chose someone else over me. And that's a hard pill to swallow when I've never felt this much for any person before him. It's all come on so fast that I haven't even had time to process how crazy it is to be fawning over a man I barely know.

I head into the bathroom and take some calming breaths. I splash my face with water. I tell myself to get a grip. And then, with my stomach full of knots, I tell myself it's time to go back to the table. I open the door to the ladies bathroom and walk straight into someone.

Oliver.

He's breathing hard as though he's just been for a long run. Was he waiting for me here? Is the look in his eyes fear or desperation? Maybe both?

Before I can say a word, his lips crash into mine, his hands tangling into my hair. I'm so shocked that I barely register it for a moment, but for once, my heart decides to rule my head. I wrap my arms around his neck and pull him out of sight into the women's bathroom.

My back hits the sink, sending a shooting pain through my spine, but I barely notice it, lost in Oliver's embrace. I know I shouldn't be doing this. It's a betrayal to Violet. It's a betrayal of my morals. But I never take anything for myself. Now, I really don't think I could refuse him if I tried.

I shift so that I'm sitting on the sink and wrap my legs around his waist, pulling him in closer to me. As our kiss deepens, I can feel his member pressing against me through his jeans. He moans quietly against my lips and I feel myself melt. I've never wanted something more.

Oliver pulls away from me and my first instinct is to pull him back in, but now that our lips aren't locked together, some of my sense is returning to me. He backs away, running a hand through his hair. I can tell by the look in his eyes that he's having second thoughts. My heart drums against my chest painfully. Did I do something wrong?

"I...there's something I need to do," he says to me, unable to look me in the eye. "I...I need to go. I'll see you soon."

And then he leaves. I stare at his back as he walks away, wondering whether he means that. Is he just saying that as an excuse to leave me here? I press my hand to my chest to feel my heartbeat. When I feel it thumping against my palm, I know this is real. It wasn't a dream or a figment of my imagination. And I never would have walked away from a kiss like that.

So how did he do it so easily?

CHAPTER SIX

Oliver

Walking away from Willow was the hardest thing I've ever had to do. I should have stopped to explain myself, to tell her why I've been so all over the place. But I know I owe it to Violet to end this thing now. I need her to see that we can't take this any further. I can see now that we should have called this off before it even started.

I'm hard as hell and I can still feel Willow's lips on mine as I hurry back to my table. I didn't want Violet to start wondering where I was when I was busy kissing Willow in the middle of the ladies' bathroom. I came here with the intention of telling Violet that it's over between us, to show her some respect and to make it clear it was never going to happen with us. Well, I've shot that concept down with what I've just done. But I have to control myself. I can't start something with Willow with a good conscience when I haven't broken things off with Violet. As much as my body is protesting leaving Willow behind, there's nothing I can do until I've come clean.

It's time to face the music now. I can't keep putting this off. I've spent this entire dinner just listening to Violet talk, wishing things were easier between us, wishing that I didn't have to do this. But I got myself into this situation. I let this go on for such a long time, knowing our arrangement needed to have an expiration date. But now that it comes to it, I know it's going to hurt.

I get back to the table and ask for the bill right away. Violet smiles and reaches out for my hand.

"What's the rush? Let's stay, have another drink…"

"No," I say, the comment coming out much harsher than I intended. "I'll walk you home…"

It was a mistake to bring her out. I was being selfish, wanting to avoid her blowing up at me when she has every right to be upset. No, we can't do it here. I need to do this somewhere where she feels safe. She doesn't seem to have a clue that something's up, so she carries on chatting as I walk her back painfully slowly. Her ridiculous shoes are halving our normal speed, but I keep pace with her. I feel a pang of pain every time I look at her eager face, the smile behind her eyes as she talks. She's trying harder than ever to impress me and it hurts knowing that I can't feel the way for her that I think she does for me. Life would've been simpler if I could just love Violet…but I don't.

I don't love Willow either, but I think I could, if I gave it a chance. Something new and exciting is blossoming between us. That kiss we shared had me coming apart in seconds. Just the thought of her now brings butterflies to my stomach. I want to kiss her again. I want to know how she feels with her body against mine. I want her in my apartment, her clothes on my bedroom floor, her smell lingering on my pillow after she leaves. I want silly things too. I want to help her dye her hair every few weeks and eat Chinese takeout in bed with her. I want to drink and dance with her and help her nurse her hangover the day after. I want the real deal. Finally, I've had my first craving for it, and now I can't get it out of my head.

I'm going to ask her on a date. Once the storm has passed following tonight with Violet, I'll take her somewhere. We can do anything she wants, just as long as she's willing to spend time with me. I hope she wasn't worried that I left in such a hurry. I hope she cares that I did. I hope she knows why I had to go…

My mind is crowded with fearful thoughts of how much tonight has and will change things, but I just need to see it through. As we finally reach Violet's student house, silence falls between us and I feel the ache of nerves even more. She turns to me with a sweet smile on her face, chewing her thumb anxiously.

"Well…you coming in or what?" she asks me. I shake my head.

"Violet…there's something I want to talk about."

"Can't it wait?" she asks, refusing to look me in the eye. "Don't ruin a good night, yeah?"

"Tonight…tonight was about trying to tell you something. I'm sorry, Violet, but I just need to get this off my chest…"

"You said we could hang out tonight. Come on…we can just watch a movie. Leave whatever it is until the morning." She leans in and tries to kiss me, but I pull away. I wish I hadn't. The look on her face is so upset that I'd do anything to make it better. But I can't. I can't carry on with this when I know things have changed. I don't love her the way she deserves to be loved.

"Violet...I don't think we should carry on seeing each other...like this."

Her sweet smile turns into anger. "Excuse me?"

"You're my best friend...and I just want to keep it that way. When we started hooking up, I thought it was simple between us...but I think the further along we go...the more complicated it's getting."

"So you just decided to take me on a date to get my hopes up? What the hell is wrong with you?"

I cover my face with my hands. This is backfiring so badly. I thought I was doing the right thing, putting us on neutral ground, but now I can see how ridiculous the idea was. Here she is, standing in front of me, looking absolutely beautiful after making such an effort...and I have to tell her that it's not enough to make me feel something for her.

"I didn't intend it to be a date...I think you misunderstood my intentions this evening. And I'm so sorry for that, I really am. But you know we can't keep on like this, Violet...I don't feel the way you want me to feel."

Violet falls silent, her lips pressed together in a thin line. I can see the tears she's trying to hold back. I try to reach for her, but she silently turns her back on me and gets out her house keys.

"I'll see you around, Oliver."

"Violet, I'm sorry, I never wanted-"

She steps inside and shuts the door in my face before I can finish my sentence. My heart jolts at the loud bang the door makes. I press my palm up against the door, willing her to open it again, but she's gone.

The whole thing couldn't have gone much worse. It's done now, but I don't feel any kind of relief. All I feel is guilt, and the crushing sensation of losing my best friend over something that should've been avoidable. I shouldn't ever have indulged in the sexual side of our relationship. I should've stayed away, made our friendship neutral and placid. All those nights we spent together were the kind of fun that I'll never forget, but at the end of it all, I've hurt her. I was selfish to only think of the ways in which this affected me.

And now I might've lost her forever.

Willow

I feel like an idiot. I just spent the past few days trying to get over the first kiss me and Oliver had. Now, it's going to take me even longer to recover from this.

I came out of the bathroom and found that Oliver was already gone, and there was no sign of Violet. I guess he's gone home, feeling guilty, but secure in his place with her. It makes me feel like shit, knowing I'm coming between the pair of them and I keep letting it happen. Plus to make matters worse, I'm still stuck on this date, seemingly with no escape.

It seems like hours before we settle the bill - he insists that he won't ever allow a woman to pay for a date and with twenty quid to my name, I have to swallow my pride. There's a cold chill in the air as we head outside and I wrap my arms around myself. My date tries to take it as an invitation to lean in closer to me, rubbing my arms to try and get some warmth into my frozen skin.

"How about you come home with me and I'll warm you up?" he murmurs. I take a step back from him, suddenly repulsed. I thought at the beginning of this evening that I'd say yes. I thought I'd be happy to go home with this good looking man, but his name still escapes me and Oliver's is etched into my mind like a tattoo. What's the point when it's not sex I'm craving? It's the familiarity of a person. It's *him* I'm craving. I shake my head and offer a polite smile to him.

"Not tonight...I think I'm just going to head home."

"So let me walk you back...maybe I can come in for a few hours."

"I don't think so. Thank you for tonight, I had a nice time. Goodnight…"

The man scoffs at me as I try to turn away. "Wow. I thought you were going to be more fun than this…but you're completely frigid. No offence."

I raise an eyebrow, feeling unscathed by his comment. "No offence, but there's not a single thing about you that interests ms. Thank you for the evening, but I think this is where it ends for us. I hope you find what you're looking for."

Leaving him behind looking like a deflated balloon, I head for home. I should've known he'd be like the rest of the men I seem to attract; sex-starved and bitter about rejection. I guess he's not the only one. I'm feeling a little like that myself now that Oliver's left me behind once again. When will I learn? I need to stop chasing someone who is going to have me up and down like a yo-yo. I guess I've been lonely for so long that I'm willing to put myself through all this for someone who doesn't deserve me. I tell myself that as I hug myself for warmth, repeating it like a mantra. *He doesn't deserve me. He doesn't deserve me. And* I *don't deserve* him. I don't deserve to be kept a dirty little secret, to be some plaything for a selfish rich boy who only thinks about himself. I feel like maybe I'm missing some of the story, and yet if he's not going to tell me it, I have to write it for myself. No good ever comes from this kind of messy behaviour. I should know better.

I catch a bus back home, wincing as I pay for it. I don't feel like walking back in the dark tonight. I close my eyes and relive the kiss I shared with Oliver, even though I know I shouldn't. It's safer in the recesses of my memory than ever letting the scenario play out again. It can't do any harm when it's not actually happening…it's just a private fantasy that doesn't hurt anyone or count as an infidelity on Oliver's part. If I concentrate, I swear I can still smell his cologne. I can still feel his hot breath on my lips and his hard member pressed against me. I'm wet just at the thought and when I open my eyes, I'm blushing. If anyone on this bus knew the thoughts I'm having, I'd never be able to go out in public again from embarrassment. I've never been like this before. Now, I feel like I'll never go back to the way I was again.

But this is ridiculous. I can go home tonight and fantasize all I like. I can spin myself some ridiculous story to delve into. I can tell myself that he's going to show up in the middle of the night, somehow climb up to the fourth floor and in through my window to have passionate sex with me. I can picture the places he'd kiss me and the words he'd whisper in my ear. It would be easy to lose myself in the idea of him, but the reality isn't so smooth. No man's perfect, but it's clear to me that Oliver has issues. Anyone willing to keep kissing a near-stranger instead of their girlfriend must be deeply unhappy and insecure. I know that as a fact.

And yet, I still want it.

CHAPTER SEVEN

Oliver

It's been three days since I last spoke to Violet or Willow, and it feels like I'm in trouble. I've tried several times to get in contact with Violet, just to make sure she's okay, but I can tell she doesn't want to speak to me. I can't blame her really, but I just want to know where I stand. I guess that's kind of selfish when she'd been wondering the same thing for the duration of our sexual relationship, so I should just keep my head down and bear the torture.

Still, it's making my life more difficult. I can't talk to Willow properly until the situation with Violet is resolved. I drafted a hundred messages to her. I wondered all weekend if she was thinking of me the way I've been thinking of her. I hope she has, and not in a bad way. I hope she's realized that I have to make things good with Violet before I can take her out on a proper date. I've also spent all weekend thinking about where I'd take her, what we'd eat, what we'd talk about...but I won't make any kind of move until Violet's okay. She's my best friend, after all, even if our relationship has taken a hit because of me. I can't let a girl I don't even know properly yet distract me.

But damn, I'm looking for a distraction.

Today's going to be a difficult one to navigate. It's my first lecture with them both since the night at the restaurant. The one saving grace of the day is that my other friends are still acting fine with me, so it seems like Violet's kept our argument to herself. I plan to try and sit with her and see how things go. I'd like to speak to Willow after class if I can too, but if not, I guess I'll catch her at the coffee shop later and explain why I've been avoiding her. She's a smart, sensitive girl. I know she'll understand.

It's the first time I've been on time for a 9am lecture in some time, and I catch sight of Willow right away. Her blue hair is a thing of beauty, and it catches my eye right away. She's sitting in her usual position on the far side of the hall, alone. There's even a bag on the seat next to her, like she's hoping to ward people away from her.

But then she catches my eye. She smiles. And then, without a word, she moves the bag from her seat and I feel my cheeks turning red.

She was saving a seat for me.

A hand clamps on my shoulder. I jolt in surprise at the physical contact and when I turn, I see Violet's face, hardened and emotionless, staring back at me. I blink several times.

"Violet…"

"You look like you weren't expecting to see me," Violet says with an edge to her tone. She's making it clear she's still not happy with me, then. But knowing Violet, she'll want to put on a united front. As much as she loves gossip, she doesn't like to be the center of drama and she certainly doesn't let herself seem rattled by anyone or anything. Especially not by me.

"Of course I was expecting to see you. At least, I was hoping to," I respond quickly. "I just-"

"The lecture is about to start. Sit," Violet says bluntly, turning her back and striding to our usual chairs. I glance back at Willow, who still looks hopeful. I wish I could go and sit with her. We could spend the next hour pretending to listen to the tutor while reading excerpts of each other's work on our laps. Or we could whisper about our favorite books, or imitate the tutor in funny voices, or even talk about what happened the other night.

Or maybe I'd just reach out and hold her hand and we'd sit quietly for the whole lecture that way. That's what I really want.

But if I walk away now, it'll be like stabbing Violet in the back. So I shoot Willow sorrowful eyes and take a seat next to Violet. Her presence is icy cold, but she gives me an approving nod. I know I've made the right decision. She wants to get our friendship back on track, I can tell. She's just going to take some time to warm up to the idea, so I need to put in the hours and be a good friend to her.

But who is being a good friend to Willow?

Willow

Watching Oliver take his seat next to Violet hurts. It hurts because I was certain that something would change today. I'd hyped myself up to the idea that it would. Oliver said he had to take care of some stuff, which I accepted after a few hours. I made myself be patient, to wait until I saw him before making a judgement. But it feels like he's thrown that back in my face now. As he sits down beside Violet, I get the sense that he's made an unspoken choice. It's her over me.

I don't know what I expected. They've got three years of history between them. Me and Oliver…our relationship is only just beginning to form, and I have no idea what he wants it to be. Does he see me as a casual fuck buddy that he might pick off the shelf some day when he's bored? Or is he looking for something more, and he just has no idea how to express himself?

I watch him through the entire lecture, paying no attention to the tutor despite my interest in poetry. I can see the tension in his shoulders. He looked as though he felt bad when he left me sitting here alone. But he's surrounded by friends. I'm the one drowning in my own solitude. We live life on entirely separate paths, and yet I'm so desperate for ours to cross that it feels like I'd do anything to make it happen. He's the one thing in my life that feels exciting right now. He keeps my heart racing and my stomach in knots and my mind jumping between euphoria and pain. This is the kind of feeling that poets write about, but I couldn't be further from wanting to write now. For once, I want to put down my pen and just live. I want to experience life with Oliver Bachelor.

But reality hits as the lecture ends and I have to dash out of the back door to the lift so I can get to my shift at the coffee shop. I hastily put my apron on over my head and get behind the counter, knowing that I might have to face Oliver at any minute. He and his friends always come here, after all, and I'm not sure I'm ready to speak to him yet. I feel flushed and sweaty at the thought of him walking in here, looking as perfect as he always does and surrounded by his friends that don't even like me. Especially Violet. I wonder how much she knows. I wonder what the deal between them is now. I'm still unsure what they mean to one another, and I feel like I deserve some clarity at this point. But I'm not going to push anything. He can come to me. I think he needs to be the one to fix this for us.

But when he shows up this afternoon, he's not with his usual posse. In fact, he's alone. He has a guilty look on his face and I immediately muster up some sympathy for him. I know better than anyone that the more connections you make with people, the more complicated life becomes. Our new found friendship has complicated things considerably, and I know from the look on his face that he's struggling. He's either ruined something good with Violet or he's looking for an escape from her. Either way, I can sympathize. He's young and stupid, like the rest of us muddling our way through university. None of us have all the answers yet, but I suspect he's coming here to try and fix the mess he's made. That, I can admire. I only hope this doesn't hurt as much as I think it might.

As he approaches the counter, I brace myself for whatever he's going to tell me. I'm scared that he'll tell me that he doesn't want me. I'm scared that he'll tell me that he does, and I'll have to start opening myself up to him and breaking down my walls. I swallow. This is out of my hands either way. I'm a big girl. I can handle whatever he has to say to me.

He stands in front of me and opens his mouth to speak, but nothing comes out. He looks tired today, now that I see him up close. I offer him a small smile.

"You want your usual?"

Oliver meets my eyes and he smiles a little. "Thanks...but maybe something stronger today. An espresso would be great, please."

"Okay."

I turn my back on him to make the drink and give him some time to gather his thoughts. He's nervous, and I don't envy him right now. Everything has been so strange between us since we kissed for the first time. Hell, the second kiss turned everything upside down. Now, we're faced with the awkwardness of reality, and I can tell he's as unprepared as I am. There's no queue behind him, so as I push his coffee toward him, he hovers, his expression one of uncertainty. Then, after a long moment, he meets my eyes.

"Things are...complicated," he tells me. I nod. "Sure."

"Things with Violet...they're delicate. And I want to talk to you properly...somewhere outside of work or class. I'd like to see you...alone."

My heart skips a beat. I imagine him and me alone at my flat. I think I could drown out the sounds of the surrounding apartments if I had the chance to get lost in his voice, in his kiss, in his embrace. Or maybe for once, we'd be the noisy ones. I blush at the thought. Some thoughts are too dirty to have at work...

"What do you think? Can we meet up and talk about it?" he asks, a tinge of desperation in his voice. He glances over his shoulder, seeming a little twitchy. And then it clicks. He knows his friends are going to show up at any minute now. He knows he's going to get caught talking to me. Maybe that's embarrassing to him, I don't know. It makes my stomach twist with frustration. He cares so much about what other people think of him, when I'm right here, trying to appreciate him, flaws and all. Is that why he's drawn to me? Because I'm seeing good in him when he's not as perfect as he pretends to be?

This boy is becoming frustrating to me. I don't know how to be around him. I sigh, leaning against the counter.

"Look, I'd like to meet up, but I have to work. I have a freelancing project to work on when I get home...I don't know when I'll be able to fit it in."

It's the honest truth. It's also my way of backing off, I guess. Like I said...making connections with people is complicated. I like him, but I don't know if I'm ready for his kind of complicated in my life. As though things aren't difficult enough without him stirring up more trouble.

But my rejection seems to hurt him. His whole face seems to droop like a wilting flower. He fiddles with the espresso cup, not looking me in the eye.

"Look, I know I've dragged you into all this...but I came here to speak to you because I like you. I want to see where things could go with us," he says, still not looking at me. "I just wanted a chance to explain everything to you...but if you're too busy to hear me out, fine."

"I didn't mean-"

"It's okay. I understand. This is a huge mess to take on," he cuts in, looking embarrassed. "I shouldn't have come here...I'm sorry. I won't bother you anymore."

Before I can protest, he leaves some money on the counter and leaves without drinking his coffee. If I wasn't working, I'd run after him. I made a mistake in trying to push him away, but I wish he could understand that I wasn't lying to him. My life is crammed full, and there's so little room for someone else in it that I've stopped trying to find it.

But he's made me want to store each spare second in the day up to put aside for him. He's made me want to give up everything else in order to have five minutes of his time. I don't want to let these new, exciting feelings go. I want to be like everyone else.

But the fact is that I'm not. Maybe it would be best if I let this go...but I'm not sure I can.

Maybe I need to give this one more go.

Tonight, when I get home, I'll try and explain what's going on. I'll do my best to build a bridge, if it's not too late.

And maybe, just maybe, things will work out the way I want them to for once.

CHAPTER EIGHT

Oliver

I was meant to hang out with my friends after speaking to Willow, but I didn't feel like it so I headed home and tried to write. I spent an hour staring at my computer screen, waiting for something to happen. I was full of emotion and I thought it would be the perfect fuel to make me write, but it had the opposite effect, draining me until I felt empty.

After some time trying, I eventually put my laptop away and lie on my bed with my eyes closed. I want to speak to one of my siblings, or preferably all of them, but I feel like I'll be bothering them by doing so. It feels like I should hold back on my own issues when I know that each of them has their own stuff going on. It feels selfish to fill up all their time with my problems.

Normally, I'd speak to Violet, but of course, that won't work this time around. She's the main issue, really. I know that she'll never be happy with me pining after anyone, but her. I know that she will be hurt to see me around anyone else. And I get it. If she feels the same way I feel toward Willow, then I know how painful the thought of her with someone else is. I guess that's what Violet thinks when she considers the possibility that I might end up with someone that isn't her.

I also want to talk to Willow now that I've calmed down, but it hurt watching her push me away again. I've made myself vulnerable in order to get to her, something I'm not used to doing. But I know I'm being selfish, expecting her to keep giving me chances when I've been nothing, but erratic since our first kiss. If only she'd said yes to giving me some time to explain myself, we could maybe move past it. But she had every right to tell me she was too busy for me. I guess now I just need to live with the fact that it's never going to happen between us.

As I lie in bed, I put my phone on my chest and wait for someone to contact me. I didn't mention that I wasn't showing up to our writer's circle today, but no one has bothered to chase me up. Maybe they know about what happened between me and Violet after all. I wonder what she's told them. I guess I'm the villain of her tale, though I never meant for that to happen. Maybe I deserve that. But the thought that I might've lost my friends all in one fell swoop makes this whole day even more depressing. I know that I'm being self-pitying and I hate it, but on days like this, I think I could just lie back and let the misery consume me entirely.

I've always struggled with my emotions. I always feel things in excess. When I'm at my happiest, which is a rare occasion these days, I feel like nothing could ever knock me off my pedestal. I'm consumed by confidence, almost cocky in my reactions to the world around me. At times like that, words fly beneath my fingers and I can type for hours without stopping, writing some of my wildest and most interesting stories. I'll run on empty, needing less sleep than usual and feeling no pressure to replace lost hours with caffeine overdoses.

But when my lows hit, sometimes weeks pass by where I'm low and angry at the world. Every little thing annoys me. I never want to get out of bed. I forget to eat and lose weight until I can feel my bones protruding from my ribcage and I have to remind myself to start buying groceries again. I neglect my writing, and sometimes my friends. Usually, I push through, knowing that if I disappear for a few weeks, my friends will likely move on and forget me. It's that simple in their world. Those who can't keep up get left behind. And as I lie here now, I realise how unimportant I am to them all. I realise that I've built my foundation for happiness on a bunch of people only interested in keeping up appearances. Some day, when we leave university and go our separate ways, we'll all just stop talking all together, and I'll have the sense to know it's nothing personal. It won't matter to them because I never mattered in the first place.

It's a dark place to be on a midweek afternoon. So when the phone finally buzzes on my chest, it feels like a defibrillator has just shocked me back to life. I try not to over excite myself as I check to see who has messaged me. And when I see who the message is from, my heart suddenly soars.

Willow actually messaged me. I can't believe it. I thought I'd never hear from her again. I guess that's a little dramatic, but with all the tension in the air, it seems like a strange time for her to message me. I open up her text and find an entire paragraph in front of my eyes.

Hey, Oliver. I feel really bad about how things panned out before. I think I was trying to push you away a little at first, but not because I don't want to get to know you. My life is kind of complicated, as you might have gathered, and sometimes I get scared about letting other people in. This is way more honest than I intended to be, but I like you, and I don't want to miss the chance of something good.

I don't know what your deal with Violet is, but I'd like to. I want to talk this over. But I meant what I said about work. I freelance as well as my shifts at the coffee shop and I struggle a lot with time. That's why I never tend to show up to events etc.

So I really am sorry, but I don't know when I'll have time to talk. I don't know if that puts you off...but if you're willing to wait, I'll wait as patiently as I can to speak with you again.

The final words in her message set my heart aflame. It feels so personal. In my head, we're both staring at clocks, our bodies multitasking while our hearts and our eyes are set on the ticking of time. But I'm far too impatient. Now that I know she's not given up on me and her, I need to find some other solution. I need to find a way to see her.

I can feel my hands shaking with anticipation as I message her back.

I'm so glad you messaged me...I've been thinking about you. How about a study date tonight? Or I can help you with your freelancing? I understand if not, I know you're busy...I just want to see you.

I hit send before I can chicken out and wait anxiously, feeling every single beat of my heart against my ribcage. I've never been like this before. Even when I was younger and I had a new girlfriend every few months, no one made my heart race like this. For once, it feels like there's something at stake if things go wrong, and I've only shared a few kisses with her.

But Willow is different. She likes the same things as me. She's got the body of a goddess. She's smart and level-headed and reasonable while I can be erratic and wild. She balances me out and brings out the side of me that I wish I brought out more around my friends. I'm starting to realize that the company I keep isn't half as good as spending a few precious minutes in her company.

Isn't this what love is meant to feel like?

Of course, I'm not in love with her. We don't know one another well enough, but there's potential here, I know there is. I can see past our first dates and to a place where we hang out comfortably without pressure, without awkwardness, and without pain. I can see happiness in a future we haven't laid the paving stones to yet. But maybe tonight...maybe tonight could be one step toward that.

She doesn't reply for some time, and it only makes me feel more anxious. I wonder if maybe I've put too much pressure on her too fast. But as the sky begins to darken outside, my phone buzzes once again and I take a deep breath, feeling the need to brace myself for whatever the text says.

A study date could work...so long as studying actually happens! Come over whenever you're ready.

I grin to myself. My bad mood has come to an immediate end as I throw myself out of bed and toward my wardrobe. I want to look good, even if it's a study date. After all, I've got a lot to live up to. The first time we kissed, we were at a party. The second time, we were both looking our best to eat at the restaurant. When she opens the door, I want the first thing she thinks to be that I look good tonight. Her opinion is the only one that matters to me, but it matters way more than it should. I've never felt the need for someone else's approval to feel myself, but now, I feel like that's changed for her.

I shower quickly and throw on a casual shirt and my best aftershave. I don't want to look like I've tried too hard, but I know this shirt is always a winner. I shove my wallet in my jeans and grab my laptop so that I can at least pretend to study while she's working. Then, with her address saved on my phone, I head out. It's not too far, but from the address she's given me, it's obvious that she's not living in the student housing.

As I approach her flat, the street seems darker and more sinister. The road is dotted with seedy looking takeaways and bars with groups of men huddled in the doorways, smoking. I've never ventured up this way before and it feels like I stick out here. Violet once told me she could sense my privilege a mile off, and it filled me with guilt. I've always known that I'm better off than most, but coming to places like this, I can see why Willow has clashed with me over my attitude to money in the past. I'm luckier than so many people, and I've never once appreciated that.

But she makes me want to be better. She makes me want to understand people more. I want to show her that I'm not just some stuck up white boy. I'm going to grow. I'm going to be a better man.

And I want her to be around to see it.

Willow

Since I sent Oliver the text telling him to come over, I haven't been able to concentrate one bit. I told myself that I wouldn't allow things to get out of hand tonight. I told myself that I'd hear him out and then keep working. I told myself to have some self-restraint, for my own sake.

But now that I know he's coming here, I can't help overthinking everything. I sprayed some cheap perfume in the air in the hopes of making the place more homely. I opened the curtain to let some light in because there's only one dim bulb to light the room. I felt like my breath might smell so I brushed my teeth twice. I thought the flat might look a little drab so I spent a good ten minutes trying to spruce the place up, knowing that his own place is much nicer than here.

And what if he's put off by this place and the way I live? There are dark yellow patches on the wall, the carpet is frayed and one of the windows has been boarded up since I moved in. If even I don't feel at home here, how will he react to my surroundings? I feel suddenly ashamed, as though I don't work hard to afford this place myself and feed myself well and put clothes on my own back. Why should I be made to feel this way just because someone richer than I'll ever be is coming over to my flat?

I push all my negative thoughts aside. He's the one who wanted to come here. He's the one who has been chasing me while I've sat back and waited to see what will happen next. He wouldn't do that if he didn't have an active interest in me. I need to stop putting myself down. Whatever his reason is for coming here, it's something good. For once, I'll get something good.

When I get the text from him telling me he's outside, I check my hair once before heading out to meet him.

Oliver looks too damn good right now. He's just wearing a pair of gray jeans and a soft-looking black jumper, but the ease of the way he wears it makes the whole thing so much better. His hair is messy, but deliberately so. His backpack is slung lazily over one shoulder like he's just rushed out of the house, and he's holding a pizza box in one hand. It's like he's tried hard to look like he doesn't care, but the effect is the opposite. He looks like he's trying to impress someone.

He's trying to impress *me*.

He smiles, aiming for his usual cocky attitude, but falling short of the mark. "Hey. Can I come in?"

"That's why you're here, isn't it?" I say, biting back a smile. He looks hesitant as he steps into the hallway. Down here, in the entrance hall, it stinks of cigarette smoke and fast food. I glance at him, looking for any sign on his face of disgust, but he doesn't say or do anything. He doesn't even have a slight wrinkle in his nose. It kind of seems like he hasn't even noticed the state of the hallway, with leaflets strewn on the floor and the muddy footprints leading to various flat doors. He's only looking at me.

"I brought sustenance…I didn't know if you'd eaten yet…or what you'd like to eat toppings wise…so I just got cheese pizza."

"You really didn't have to…" I tell him. I don't have much experience with men outside of one night stands, and yet this feels like the closest I've been to receiving flowers. It's not a romantic gesture, exactly, but it's a sign he's been thinking about me. The pizza smells good, and it feels like a peace offering. He shrugs like it's nothing, because to him, it is. But to me, it really does mean something.

"I thought it would be nice...study sessions are lame without some snacks to get distracted by."

"Well...that's really nice of you. Thank you."

He shrugs again, and his cheeks look a little red. Is Oliver really blushing?

"Lead the way…"

I feel nervous as he follows behind me up the stairs. I'm aware from this angle that he can see every inch of me and I can't even turn to see if he's looking. It makes me feel like I'm on display, and I can't tell if I like that or not. I want him to notice me...and yet I feel too shy to relax about it. Shyness isn't my thing, though. It never has been, and I'm not going to allow a man to knock my nerves, even if it's for all the right reasons.

I can feel my fingers trembling as I fumble with my keys, but I tell myself to get a grip. He waits patiently, his shoulder leaning against the wall beside the door. He's watching me as though I'm doing something very interesting. That explains the nerves, I guess; it's like he's expecting me to put on some kind of show for him, as though I'm meant to be intriguing to him all the time. Rich boys like shiny things, I suppose. I glance at him with a raised eyebrow.

"Did you come prepared to study?"

He shrugs. "I brought my laptop."

"Good. I've got a million and one things to do…"

"Don't let me stop you," he says, a playful smile on his lips. I wish he *would* stop me, but I can't cave so easily to that smile. He still has some explaining to do, and I have work up to my eyeballs. If he came here expecting me to give in to a little flirting, then he's going to be in for a shock.

As I open the door to the flat, I stride in with as much confidence as I can muster. I keep my chin high, hoping I look proud of my place here. If I see it as a palace, maybe he will too.

But he doesn't even look at the apartment. His eyes are fixed on me. He hovers for a moment, not knowing what to do with himself. It surprises me to find that he's polite. He's waiting to be invited to sit down. Plus, while he's been standing waiting for me to take the lead, he's slid off his trainers and tucked them neatly beneath the coffee table. I guess he's used to being in the kinds of places where a grubby shoe print on the carpet is much more of a disaster.

"Where shall we work? The sofa? The desk? The bed?"

I blush. He says it completely innocently, but the thought of being in proximity to a bed with him just takes me straight back to the night at his party when we kissed for the first time.

"We can work on the sofa. And maybe grab a slice of pizza before it gets cold..."

He grins. "I like that logic."

I'm giving myself a total of ten minutes for this. I need to hear him out, and I can tell he's ready to talk. I still have a lot to do this evening, but him coming here is important too. For once, I need to put my social life first, just for a while. Plus, I'm starving.

He sits down and opens the box of pizza, offering me the first slice. We eat in silence for a moment and he demolishes his first slice, not bothering to reach for another. He turns his body toward me, his posture a little stiff. It's like he's forgotten how to sit normally, thrown off by his new environment and the change in company. I guess things are more straight-forward with Violet. He clears his throat.

"So...I just wanted a chance to explain myself. First of all...I don't want you to think I'm a cheat. I know that a lot of people think that me and Violet are a couple...and I guess we've always acted a little like we are. But we were never together. We've been kind of...well…"

"Casual?"

He nods, looking slightly embarrassed. "We agreed that if things got too intense, or if one of us found someone, then it'd be over. I thought it was simple in that respect...we'd laid down some rules, you know? And for me, I never felt like there was a risk of me falling for her. I assumed she felt the same. But feelings don't necessarily follow the rules...so I suppose that was naive on my part. I know a lot of people think it's a dumb thing to do, starting a casual relationship with your friend, and now that it's over-"

"It's over?" I say in surprise. I wasn't expecting him to say that. After all, he doesn't owe me anything. It would be easy enough for him to fall back on what he and Violet have instead of starting something fresh. But he nods at me.

"Yeah. I never really took it seriously, if I'm honest. I feel terrible saying that now, given the circumstances. It took me a really long time to realize that she and I saw the arrangement in different ways. In fact, I had no idea until very recently that she felt…well, that she wanted it to be real. For me, it was good company…a way to feel less alone…and for her, it was like a preamble to something more."

I nod slowly. It's obvious to me as an outsider that these things get complicated the second feelings get involved. But maybe Oliver was blissfully unaware of what he was getting himself into. And with Violet's feelings involved, it makes complete sense to me now why he sat with her in the lecture and not me. It's not because he's a player.

It's because he's trying to be a good friend.

"Did things…are things alright between the two of you?"

He sighs, running a hand through his hair and ruffling it even more. "Well, I wouldn't say that…but I think, given time, she'll be okay. She just needs me to not make a big deal of it. She needs us to pretend that everything is normal until eventually, it is. That's why…well, I've been trying to keep my distance from you when I can. Because I know it'll hurt her to see me with you."

"I get it."

"It's not fair on you though, Willow. I've dragged you into the middle of something you shouldn't be involved in. But selfishly, I can't seem to help myself. I'm drawn to you. I don't want to be apart from you. I want to be able to see you." He shakes his head. "I'm not good at this…"

"You're doing fine," I tell him. I shuffle a little closer to him. "Look…life is complicated. I know that better than a lot of people. But if you want this to be a thing…then it can be. And it doesn't need to happen right this second…there's no rush. I don't need you to get down on one knee, Oliver. I'm happy just to hang out when we have time…we can take it easy. See where it goes," I tell him. I can't believe I've managed to keep my voice so level when my heart is beating so fast. I care a lot more than I'm letting on, but in truth, I had no idea how much I was feeling until these words came spilling out of my mouth. I want to date him. I want to kiss him when I feel like it. I want to not tread on eggshells.

But I feel strongly enough that I'm willing to wait. Even though it feels torturous to be kept dangling like this, I'm willing to put myself through it because this matters. If he was unimportant to me and my life, I'd give up easily. I have bigger issues than worrying about a guy and all of his baggage at the same time. But with Oliver…it feels different. It feels worth waiting.

Oliver's face is unreadable for a moment as he takes in everything I've said to him. Maybe he thinks I'm not that bothered about the whole thing. I've certainly made a point of playing it cool this evening. But I want him to know that I do care. And when he smiles at me, I smile back.

"Okay…taking it easy it is," he says.

"Just to be clear, though…taking it easy does *not* mean casual. If you want to date me, then you're dating me. I don't like to be messed around."

"I wouldn't," Oliver says softly. "That's the last thing I want to do."

"Good. Because I won't stand for it," I say firmly. As much as I want this, I have to protect my heart somehow. Maybe I'll loosen the reins when he's given me more of a reason to trust him. But for now, I'm making my boundaries clear.

"I'm on your level, Willow. I'll do whatever it takes to have my shot with you."

I search his face for any signs of insincerity, but I don't find any. I'm usually good at reading people so I find my shoulders relaxing a little. I shift away from him again and grab another slice of pizza.

"Okay. Then we're good."

"So we can leave the conversation there for tonight…yeah? I don't want to get in the way of your evening."

I sigh as I take a bite of pizza. "You're not in the way…it's just I have a lot to do…"

"Is there anything I can help with?" he asks, his eyes eager. "I mean, considering I'm the best writer you know…"

I snort. "Yeah, alright, don't flatter yourself too much…but I'm not sure how you could help me, to be honest. I'm writing a romance novel for my employer-"

"What, like an entire novel? Are you serious? How do you have time for that?"

I shrug. "I turn one in once a month. Once I get started, it's not too hard to get into the swing of it…I just have to get pen to paper. But it's not like we can co-author it, is it?"

Oliver shrugs. "Well, I don't see why not…."

"What, like I dictate and you type? It'd be just as quick to do it alone…"

"Not exactly…I've had a thought. Have you got voice typing on your laptop?"

"I've never looked…"

"Let me take a look…"

I hand my laptop to him and he plays around with the settings for a bit until he finds what he's looking for. Then, he balances the laptop between us on the sofa, grinning at me as though he's just done something really impressive.

"So…when you were a kid, did you ever play that game where one of you writes a word, and then the next person has to carry it on?"

I nod tentatively. This feels like a disaster waiting to happen, but I kind of want to entertain it.

"So I was thinking...we can each speak a sentence and then carry it on between us...and since it looks like this is a romance scene...we could be one character each? And try to speak their dialogue?"

I laugh. "Wow, I'm not sure I'm drunk enough for this kind of role playing game...as in, I'm stone cold sober."

He smiles. "I'd suggest we crack open a bottle of wine, but I won't be a bad influence today, I swear...come on, it'll be fun. Think of it as a new creative angle. And perhaps a load of your shoulders?"

I should say no. After all, this process seems like it's going to mean me going back later and editing the whole thing. But I want to give in to him. I want to forget my responsibilities for a while and just enjoy his company. The whole exercise sounds ridiculous, and yet I want to entertain it, just for him.

"Alright...let's give it a go. You might want to read a few pages before and then we can start…"

He nods, taking the whole thing more seriously than I expected him too. I watch him as he reads. I've never had the pleasure of watching him read before and I have to admit, it's nice to see. He furrows his brow while he does it, absent-mindedly chewing on his thumb in concentration. Occasionally, he'll make an approving noise or nod to himself before adjusting his position on the page. When he gets up to speed, he offers me a smile.

"I've never read your romance stuff before...it's different, but I like it. It's...heart-warming."

I know he's teasing me now and I shove his shoulder, making him laugh and throw up his hands defensively.

"Alright, alright, I'm sorry...but truly, this is good. I like it a lot. Then again, I like everything you write."

I shake my head to myself. It always strikes me how easy it seems for him to give out compliments. It doesn't cost him a thing, and yet each one is worth a million. It's better than any physical gift he could give me...even a pretty delicious pizza.

"Shall I start?" he asks, clearing his throat for comic effect. "So...here goes." He clicks a button to begin the voice activation.

"...Alice's eyes were filled with doubt. Her lover was confusing to her at the best of times. Now, he was standing on her doorstep, his hair dripping from the rain, telling her that he needed her." Oliver raises his eyes to look at me, giving me permission to take up the baton. I take a deep breath. It feels strange to speak the words that are forming in my head, but I have to embrace new experiences today. I'm already out of my comfort zone. This can't be much worse.

"...His eyes looked different than they usually did. The fired up anger in his eyes had been replaced by something softer, more gentle. There was still passion there, but the look in his eyes...it was closer to a flickering candle than a giant inferno."

I can see the smile on Oliver's lips threatening to burst out. This whole thing is making me feel so vulnerable. I realise it's because it's too close to how I've felt these past few weeks with Oliver. And the way he's looking at me makes me feel so naked. Like he sees me completely as I am.

"I can't do this. I can't be without you," Oliver murmurs. It takes me a moment to remember that this is part of the game. In his eyes are the exact things I just described aloud. That calm flicker of passion is something I'm growing used to seeing, but I can't get used to the feeling it brings out in me. I take a deep breath.

"You've never said that before...you have a wife at home. This was always supposed to be something simple," I whisper. I'm certain that the computer hasn't even picked up what I said, but I don't care much. This whole game feels too close to home for it to be playful anymore. When Oliver looks me in the eyes, I can tell that he wants to do something. He wants to reach out and touch me, or say something true, or close the gap between our lips. But he pauses and silence fills the air. I imagine that I'm Alice. I imagine him standing on my doorstep with water dripping from his hair. He takes a deep breath.

"Sometimes, you can't help the way you feel," he says, blurring the lines between our reality and the story we're trying to tell. *"When I married her, I felt something for her. I really did. But meeting you...it made those feelings seem small and insignificant. I can't deny how I feel anymore...I'm so desperate for you, Alice. It's an ache inside*

me. Existence is pain without you at my side. And these things I feel...they make me cold and uncaring to the rest of the world. I could hurt any number of people for my own selfish need for happiness. I'll tear every seam of my life apart to find solid ground with you."

I can't help being shocked by the intensity of it all. This was meant to be fun, but his words are stirring something inside me. He's speaking like he knows how this feels. Either he's a good actor or he knows exactly how to get a girl to believe every word that leaves his lips.

Or he's a good writer, I suppose.

I open my mouth, but no words come out. He's moved closer without me noticing. I want to reach out and cup his cheek, so I do. Where's the sense in holding back anymore? Surely he wanted this to bring us together, and now we're mere inches apart. I close my eyes for a moment.

"...Alice's eyes fluttered up to meet her lover's once again. She could see from the way he looked at her that he meant every word he said." I open my eyes to meet Oliver's. I hear his breath catch in his throat. I can feel my heart throbbing against my chest with frightening intensity. It's now or never, I guess...

"Alice's last thought before she kissed him was of how sweet it would be to give in…"

Oliver closes the gap between us, stopping me mid sentence with his lips. His hand touches the back of my neck, tickling the skin pleasantly as he rubs his thumb over it. I lean in closer, closing my eyes and enjoying the moment. It's more like the first kiss we shared than the second. It's calm and understated, but just as good as I imagined it would be. It makes me feel like the troubled waters between us have finally calmed down. It feels natural. It feels right.

When we break apart, the primary expression on his face is surprise. It's like he wasn't expecting this moment to occur, even though this is what he came for. But his surprise soon switches to a smile.

"Can I take you out?" he asks, and though I know we're not playing the game anymore, I smile.

"Alice looked her lover deep in the eyes and considered his proposal. There was a certain amount of danger to giving in to him. Surrendering herself to her emotions was new ground for her, and it felt like everything might come crashing down on her head if she did..."

Oliver grins back, humouring me. I suppress a giggle.

"But she also knew that if she didn't say yes, she'd regret it forever. And so she cupped her lover's cheek and said..."

"Bring it on," Oliver finishes for me.

CHAPTER NINE

Oliver

I've got butterflies in my stomach this morning. I can't remember the last time I went on a date and cared about it. Back home in California, I used to date a lot. The girls I knew from school were all good friends of mine, and at the time it seemed fine that we all dated one another. It didn't mean a thing and even if there were mini-heartbreaks, they were soon forgiven and forgotten.

But today is different. I actually want this to go somewhere. I want to make Willow feel good. I want her to feel reassured that I'm the real deal.

But it's hard knowing where to begin. I don't know what I can and can't do in this situation. I'm still learning her sense of humour and how far I can push my jokes. I'm still figuring out what her beliefs are and whether they match up to mine. I'm still wondering whether this initial attraction is going to be enough to bind us together. But I guess I'll never know if I don't take a leap of faith.

We don't have any solid plans today. I told her I'd meet her outside her flat and we could go wherever we fancied. It's a little nerve-wracking not having a plan, but the nerves are worth seeing her again. Finally, we're on our own terms. Finally, we're exploring these feelings that have haunted us for these past few weeks.

I text her when I arrive outside her place and hold my breath until she answers the door. An involuntary smile springs to my mouth. She looks so good today. Her hair seems extra vibrant against her yellow pinafore dress. She's sewn on all sorts of things, as though she's putting together a jigsaw of her personality. There are several band patches that I recognise, and some I don't. There are also a few that look like tattoos, but in the form of fabric, like a rose and a skull and crossbones. It's an eclectic outfit, and it suits her perfectly. She's never worn anything like this to university, and I feel almost honoured that I'm seeing Willow at her most Willow. She looks me in the eye without shying away as she smiles at me in greeting.

"Hey…thanks for picking me up," she says.

"That's no problem…what would you like to do?"

She shrugs. "I don't mind…so long as we don't spend much. I hope that's okay…I'm just kind of perpetually short of cash."

I almost say that I'll pay for everything we do today, but I quickly realise that's a terrible idea. Not only is Willow determined to support herself, but she's also got a lot of pride. I wouldn't want her to feel like I'm taking pity on her. So instead, I smile.

"Suits me. To be honest…in all the time I've been here, I've never really done the touristy things…what do you say? Fancy taking me on a tour?"

"I don't see why not…I just never took you for the touristy type, I guess. I thought you'd want to be on a pub crawl or something."

I laugh. "Even I don't go on pub crawls in the middle of the day…often."

"Classic," she says and we easily fall in step with one another. "Well, I'm laying down one rule now…no drinks until five o'clock."

"It's five o'clock somewhere…"

"Hey, look at you. You've been off American soil too long…you're becoming a British alcoholic."

I grin in response. "Why do you think I moved here? I wasn't going to wait until I was twenty-one to drink…"

"Like you would anyway. You're not exactly one to follow the rules," she says. I can't tell if it's a compliment or not, but either way, she's smiling. I get the feeling today is going to be good. Better than I expected, even.

We head into the town center, talking about nothing in particular. It feels easy. I've always found it quite easy to find something to talk about with everyone I meet, but with Willow, there's no effort involved.

We meander past the Bombed Out Church and down Bold Street, passing by all the thrifty stores and independent restaurants. Our bodies keep brushing against each other as though a magnetic force is pulling us together. We stop for a while to watch a man with an inflatable microphone and an impressive green suit warbling a rendition of a song that seems familiar, but I can't quite place. I've seen him before around town, considering he's kind of a local legend, but walking by him with Willow, this city feels even more like home than usual.

We turn right and head toward the public library, which is somewhere I've never actually been before. When I tell Willow, she raises her eyebrow.

"You do realize our tutors took us there once, right?"

I smile sheepishly. "I might've skipped that field trip."

"Why am I not surprised," she mutters, but I can see the affection in her eyes. Is it possible that these past few weeks have softened her opinions of me?

The library is actually pretty cool. Looking up, the ceiling reminds me of the roof of a sunhouse. The smell of coffee and books is always inviting, and though we don't stay long, I can imagine Willow here, typing away on her laptop at the speed of light, inspired by the productive environment. Whenever I imagine Willow now, she's writing, and somehow, that's the best image I can conjure in this world.

After we come out of the library, we spend at least an hour in the Walker Art Gallery. Willow stands close to me as we're looking at each painting, and even though there's no signs telling us to keep quiet, she whispers as she explains the story behind each painting. I nudge her arm.

"How do you know all this stuff?"

She shrugs. "I come here quite a lot…I mean, I learned some of these stories as a kid. Our school brought us on a trip here once. But sometimes, I come during my lunch break. It's right by the library, after all. I like reading about them all. I've learned a lot."

"Wouldn't you rather hang out with someone every now and then? Like, grab a coffee with someone or something?"

Willow shrugs. "Socialization is expensive. And addictive. If I spend an hour with a person, I want to spend a day with them. And since I don't have time for that…it's easier just to be lonely than to be a half-hearted friend."

"Willow…"

"I don't choose to be a loner…it just worked out that way," she says. For the first time, I see some sadness in her eyes, but she quickly finds a way to cover up her emotions. She's clearly an expert at it. I wish I could figure out what led her to this place, but I know she's not going to open up right now, and I wouldn't want her to. I want her to have a good time today and leave her troubles behind. Before I can tell myself it's a bad idea, I slip my arm around her waist.

"Well you're stuck with me today," I murmur in her ear. She looks up at me and smiles. In a split second, she's back.

"That doesn't seem like such a bad thing to me."

From there, we take a walk around the docks and the Tate, trying to figure out whether we love or hate the modern art pieces we pass. Then I insist that we go inside the Beatles museum, even though it's a little pricey to get in. I've never been before and I say as much, so Willow relents and allows me to pay for us to go inside. I feel a little bad as we're looking through all the memorabilia and costumes and original lyric books. After all, Violet said she wanted to bring me here and I blew her off to go with someone else. But I can't help feeling like this is the right thing for me. I have to push her to the back of my mind. For once, I'm thinking about myself. For once, I don't care what anyone else says or thinks.

This is my time.

Willow

I can't claim to have been on many dates before, but this day has to trump all dates that I'll ever go on again. Spending the day just wandering around my favourite city in Oliver's company is like a dream come true. As first dates go, this one has been enchanting, and it's leaving me hungry for more...something I never expected to happen with the pompous posh boy from my lectures.

But the date isn't over yet. As mid-afternoon approaches, Oliver guides me to the waterfront once again and pays for us to take a trip along the Mersey. As much as I don't like that he's spending this money on me, I tell myself that I'll pay for whatever we do next time...if there is a next time, of course. Maybe guys like Oliver take you on one date that you know you'll never be able to forget and then leave you high and dry. I don't want to think that way, though. I'm willing to believe he's one of the good ones.

His hand slips into mine as we get onto the boat and for some reason, it shocks me. I knew we were here on a date, and yet holding his hand feels so serious. Kisses in dark rooms and sexual desires that run around your head when you're alone…those are different. Somehow, holding hands seems more intimate than anything we could do between the sheets.

The wind whips my hair as we head to the top deck of the boat. It's cold out here, but the sun is still beating down on our shoulders. Spring is well and truly here. We take a seat, our thighs pressed close together and our hands still locked. The boat sets off with only a few other tourists on board, making it easier to pretend that it's just me and Oliver here. He cranes his neck, eagerly watching the sights pass by as though he hasn't lived here for three years. A smile plays on his lips.

"This really is a beautiful city," he says, shouting to be heard over the wind. I lean close to his ear.

"It's the best." As we pass by the Liver building, I point at the two birds standing proudly on top of it. "Do you know what they say about the Liver birds?"

"Enlighten me…"

"According to local legend, the one facing the city is a man who is looking to see if the pubs are open."

"Standard."

"And the front one...apparently it's a female who is looking out to sea to see if there are any handsome sailors coming into the shore."

He turns to me with his winning smile. "Shall I give her a wave then?"

I laugh, shaking my head at him. "You think you're so smooth, don't you?"

He leans closer to me, still smiling. "And you don't agree?"

My eyes search his for a moment. I hold my breath as my heart pounds against my chest. I'm so dangerously close to something good, so close to getting what I want that it makes me anxious. But I know that I deserve something to go right. I've done things I regret, but I know in my heart I'm a good person. All I want now is someone to share myself with.

He leans in to kiss me and it takes my breath away. He's still holding my hand and his thumb brushes across the back of it as he kisses me. But the kiss is short and sweet. The kind of kiss that you give someone you've been with for a long time. It's the kind of kiss that should just feel comfortable and natural, but it's hard to imagine a kiss with Oliver being that way when he's got my heart thumping at a million miles an hour. If it's affected him, he doesn't show it, looking back out over the water as though me and him kissing is ordinary behaviour. But I've never felt more on edge. I want to grab him and kiss him again just to convince myself that this is real. I want him to show some signs of being shaken up by this. But he's cool as a cucumber, which shouldn't surprise me in the slightest. Even as his hand squeezes mine, I feel the tiniest seed of doubt planting itself in my heart.

Do I want this more than him?

"I'm glad we did this today," he says, but he's not looking at me. He's looking out to the land, just like the Liver Bird. But I'm not looking out to sea.

I'm looking at him.

We spend an hour on the boat and when we get off, my legs feel a little wobbly from the choppy waters. His arm snakes around my waist as though to steady me, and I find myself once again unable to breathe.

"Where to next?" he asks breezily. "We could head for a drink? Or we can chill at home…whatever you want."

The thought of taking him home again is a dangerous one. The things I'd do there given the opportunity would have me losing my final scrap of control. Maybe I should call it a day. Maybe this is the perfect place to end the date when everything is going so well. He tugs me in a little closer and I wish I had the confidence to kiss him right now. Out here in the open, it feels like I'm not allowed. It was different on the boat when no one cared what we were doing. Now that we're back on solid ground, I'm feeling the pressure.

"Well...I don't mind, really. I mean, it would be nice if we-"

"Oliver."

The familiar voice has my stomach in knots. I turn and see that Violet is standing a few metres away at the Pier Head. This is the worst possible person we could've run into, and I get the feeling she's about to put a stop to all the fun we're having. She looks me up and down icily as though I'm a slug that's invaded her home territory. I guess she kind of sees Oliver as hers, but it's hard to have sympathy for her when she's spent the past few weeks so determined to hate me. I've never wanted to fight with a woman over a man, but I think that's exactly what she wants me to do with her.

"Violet," Oliver says calmly. "How are you?"

"Can I talk to you?" she says, ignoring his polite small talk. "Without her?"

"Violet, you're being rude," Oliver says, but without much force. I should've expected that - he's still treading on eggshells with her -- but I wish he'd put up more of a fight for me. I roll my shoulders back, letting go of his hands. I'm forgetting one small detail.

I don't need anyone to fight for me.

"I'll go," I say quietly, immediately wishing my voice had more power to it. Oliver's eyes widen.

"Willow...we were going to-"

"It's okay. You guys need to talk things over. It's fine," I say. I really want to not be selfish about this. I know he's having a hard time over this whole thing with Violet. But I wanted him to myself today, and it feels like a stab to the heart knowing that really, he's picking her over me again. What should I expect? They have years of history and he and I are just getting started. I'm being ridiculous.

But I still wanted to come first.

Oliver tries to take my hand again, but knowing how much it'll hurt Violet, I step away. I watch his face fall, but what else was I meant to do? For a smart guy, he really is clueless about this stuff. I nod to Violet as pleasantly as I can manage.

"I'll see you guys around."

I can feel two pairs of eyes burning into the back of my head as I walk away. And with each step I take, the tears forming in my eyes sting a little more.

CHAPTER TEN

Oliver

Watching Willow walk off has left a stone in the pit of my stomach, weighing me down. Everything was going so damn perfect until Violet showed up. She might be my closest friend, but right now, she feels more like an enemy. I know we only bumped into one another by chance, but the way she just sabotaged my date is making me feel like she's on a mission to ruin everything for me. I turn to her, unable to hide the hurt from my face. She crosses her arms.

"Nice date?"

"It was," I say through gritted teeth. "Violet...whatever this is...couldn't it have waited?"

Violet has the sense to look a little guilty. "Look...I'm not trying to ruin things. I'm really not, I promise. I just thought you should know something about her...something I found out lately."

"About Willow? And since when are you an expert on her and her life? You don't even know her."

Violet sighs and rolls her eyes as though I'm the one causing trouble here. "Look, you don't have to stay. Chase her down if you want. It's none of my business. I'm trying to be a mate here. Let's go and sit down, have a drink-"

"No," I say bluntly. "We're not turning this into some kind of social occasion. I just blew her off for you because you made it seem important. She gave us grace because she knows I want to fix things with you, so if you've got something to say, say it. If it's so urgent, you can tell me here."

Violet looks shocked at my response. I don't think I've ever been so blunt with her. If only I'd mustered the courage to say that when Willow was still here. I can see her crossing over at the traffic lights now and I wish I was with her. But Violet is fumbling for something in her pocket with her lips pursed, so I wait, trying to remain patient with her. I can still see the hurt in her eyes when she looks back up at me.

"I just thought you should know...there's stuff she's keeping from you. That's what I'm about to show you."

I want to roll my eyes, but I keep my voice level as I respond. "How can you be so sure of that? She could've told me anything."

"Trust me. She didn't tell you this."

She shows me the screen of her phone and I stare at it, wondering what I'm meant to be looking at. The website looks a little seedy, like it's for something that I shouldn't be looking at. I frown and glance up at Violet.

"What is this?"

"It was Rob's birthday last night...you missed it."

"Well, yeah. It was at a strip club. You know I'm not interested in going to places like that."

"I know...this is the website for the place we went. It hasn't been updated in a while. But we found something on here that you're going to want to see..."

She scrolls through the site for a minute and then turns the screen back toward me. My heart is beating hard as I lean in to see what it is that she's showing me.

There's a black and white picture of Willow right before my eyes. She looks a little younger and her hair is longer. Her lips are painted a dark color and she's smoldering at the camera. I can't understand why I'm seeing this picture at all.

"What is this?"

"It's a gallery of the employees, Oliver. She works there...or she used to. Her photographs are hung in the club. And there's more...of her in action."

I feel a jolt right through my heart. If this is true, then this is a huge thing for her not to tell me. Granted, we're still getting to know one another, but this feels like something I should know, at least down the line. But she's told me about her job...she's always so busy with her freelancing and her cafe job...is it possible that she's been lying to me to cover her tracks?

I shake my head, trying to make sense of it all. Willow seems so upfront, so honest, so open...but now, I'm questioning everything I know about her. The evidence that she used to do this is before my eyes right now. I guess it's not my business how she makes money to live on, but I just wish she'd told me. I thought we were starting to be honest with one another.

Violet slips her phone back into her bag and eyes me up, looking for a reaction. "Well? Are you shocked?"

I take a step back from her. I can feel anger rising inside me like a volcano about to erupt. "Is that what you were hoping for? That this would be like some wake-up call to me or something? That I'd lose interest?"

"No, I just-"

"Why can't you just let me be happy?" I snap. "I've met someone that I click with. I was having a great day with her, and you've just waltzed in and tried to ruin it."

"I just thought-"

"Honestly, Violet, I don't want to hear it...I know I messed up. I know things between us are bad now, and maybe that can't be fixed. But this is a step too far, trying to shame her, trying to take it out on her like she's some cheap joke. She would *never* do the same to you, even after the way you've treated her." I pause for breath, shaking. "I'm don where. I'd really appreciate it if you left me alone for a while," I tell her, already walking away from her. She jogs to keep up with me.

"I'm being a good friend…"

I shake my head at her. "If you want to be a good friend, just back off…please. I really don't think I can be around you for now."

She doesn't follow me as I continue walking off. I'm shaking with fury. It doesn't matter to me suddenly that Willow hasn't told me about this. That's her business. But listening to Violet trying to expose her like that is a step too far. Why did she have to stick her nose in and try to make things more complicated than they already are?

I don't even know where I'm going right now. I want to talk to Willow, but I get the feeling that she's pissed off at me. And with every right. I made the choice to stay here and listen to Violet, but she's used and abused every chance I've given her. I might've messed up our friendship, but she's digging its grave even deeper.

I hear footsteps behind me and blink in surprise as I turn and see that Violet is rushing toward me. I come to a stop and she prods her finger into my chest.

"I'm not taking the blame for this," she snarls. "You led me on. You know you did. So what if I don't want you seeing someone else? You were supposed to be with me, Oliver. How do you think I felt seeing you with her today? That's why I told you."

"What, so just because you're not happy, no one can be?" I scoff. "Look, Violet, I'm so sorry if I hurt you, but I made it clear from the start-"

"Clear? You call sleeping with me twice a week clear? You call all those nights we spent together clarity? Fuck you."

There are people looking at us now and I wish I could just slip away, but this is my life. I have to face up to it. I look Violet right in the eye, breathing hard.

"Violet...I want to date Willow. I always saw you as a friend...and I'm sorry that I couldn't make myself feel more. You need someone who gives you as much love as you give out. But I can't be that person. And you can keep punishing me for that, but don't try to hurt Willow just to hurt me. Hurt me all you want, but leave her out of it. She's done nothing wrong, and I'm just doing my best to fix the mess I made. So let's pretend this conversation never happened and move on with our lives."

Walking through the centre of the town, I feel like all eyes are on me. My cheeks are heating up and my heart is racing, but I'm finally being honest with myself and everyone around me. I can't hold back anymore. I don't want my chance with Willow to be screwed up because of this.

I have to go and speak to her before it's too late.

Willow

Coming home after the date felt like returning to reality after a particularly nice dream. The real world isn't quite so inviting. I sat down on my battered sofa with a cup of coffee and told myself to forget it all. I'm putting too much pressure on him - and on myself - to make this happen, but maybe some things just aren't meant to be.

I try to continue a piece of coursework that I've started, but I can't concentrate. He's consuming my mind. I've never had much time for romance, and yet this one with Oliver has swept me off my feet. My lips are still tingling with the sensation of the kiss he left on my lips on the boat trip. Did it mean nothing to him? Is it easy for him to just dismiss this?

I want to bury my face in a pillow and scream. When you spend a lot of time alone, you find that you forget how others can make you feel. You forget the deep ache of loneliness, the sharp knife of betrayal, the keen pang of lovesickness. Now that Oliver has wormed his way into my life and my heart, everything feels amplified. Crazy as it sounds, it feels like I'm suffering from a broken heart.

I have to remind myself of the things I've endured in my life. My life before I came here to this shitty flat was a whole lot worse. The way people have treated me my whole life doesn't compare to the disinterest of a man I barely know. And yet, I feel like this matters more than anything right now. I've heard people say before that romantic feelings can send you crazy. They can make you think that the way you're feeling is the centre of all things. I guess I just never believed that until now.

My phone buzzes beside me and I ignore it, burying my face in the sofa cushions. Ten minutes later, it buzzes again. And then, with my heart aching and heavy in my chest, I hear the buzzer to my flat sound.

There's only one person who has ever visited me here, and he's the last person I want to see if he's going to make me feel worse than I already do. I force myself to get up off the sofa to answer the buzzer.

"Oliver...I really don't want to talk right now."

"Willow, I'm sorry I let you walk away...I really am. I know that must have felt lousy, but I thought I was keeping the peace…"

I close my eyes. I can't get the thought to shift from my head that he's only half into this. I don't want to put my heart on the line when I'm not certain I can get something good from it. It feels too risky after everything I've been through over the years. My heart has taken quite a beating and one last punch might finish me off. I lean my head against the wall.

"I don't want you to mess me around, Oliver, I told you that already…"

"I swear that's not my intention. I thought Violet wanted to hash things out, but I was wrong. She…she had other ideas, and I'm done with her now. I want to tell you everything and be honest with you. Please just let me come in…"

I know he's not the sort to give up easily so I sigh and press the button to allow him in. I try my best to compose myself while I'm waiting for him, but the second he arrives outside my door, I feel my heart sinking.

Oliver has his head hung and his eyes are full of pain. I want to reach out to him and hold him, but I can't let myself give in to him this easily. Since all this began, I've been allowing him to keep making things more complicated. I don't need any more complications in my life, even if they're as good as him.

"Please don't come in if you're going to mess me around more," I say. I wish I sounded more in command, but for once, my voice has failed me. Oliver raises his eyes to meet mine.

"That's not why I'm here. I promise. I…" He scratches the back of his head, looking wholly uncomfortable. "I like you…a lot. Today was the best day I've had in a long time. And I know I might've ruined that. But Willow…I swear I want this."

I scrutinize his face. I've got a good radar for liars. I know when someone isn't being honest with me. But Oliver wears his heart on his sleeve much more than I realized. He's telling the truth…and knowing that he likes me makes me want to give him one last shot.

I step aside to let him and he gives me a grateful smile before coming inside. I head to my fridge and take out two beers. I've been saving them, but I think a time like this calls for them. I hand one to Oliver and he smiles half-heartedly.

"Thanks. Look, I shouldn't have let you go earlier…I've been friends with Violet for a long time and I feel like I owe her so much…I'm scared that I led her on unintentionally. She says I did it knowingly, but I didn't. I really thought we had cracked the code, that we could just keep it friendly. But I can see how dumb that is now. I hurt her because of it, and I felt like I had to give her time to talk to me and say her piece. But it turns out she's not the person I thought she was. I think…I think she was just trying to stir up trouble for us."

I settle next to him on the sofa, feeling the tension of the day tightening my shoulders. "Stir up trouble?"

He struggles to meet my gaze. "She showed me something…and I have to admit it did shock me a bit. Willow…are you still working at the…club?"

It takes me a minute to realize what he's referring to. My heart stops for a moment and then it plummets to my stomach. Those days of working in the strip bar are so far behind me that it feels like another life. It might only have been two years ago, but I've come such a long way since then. I cover my face with my hand, needing a moment to get my thoughts together. I flinch when I feel Oliver's hand on my arm.

"Willow…we don't need to talk about it if you don't want to…and nothing has changed, I promise. I was just surprised."

"How did she find out?"

"She was at the place last night…she saw a photograph of you on the wall. And the website hasn't been updated for a while…"

I sigh, pulling at my earlobe anxiously. I have complicated feelings about working in the club. It was a hard time for me, but life had been worse beforehand. And sex work is never an easy thing to navigate as a woman. Some call it empowering, some call it gross, but the system only keeps going because people pay for it. I will never judge anyone for doing it, but it doesn't mean I don't think it's exploitative. *I* was exploited.

But I'm not ashamed. I will never feel shame for doing what I had to in order to survive at the time. It's just not ideal that the guy I'm trying to date has found out this way...especially from a girl who would seemingly do anything to try and ruin me.

But I can't hide from my past. No matter how far I run from it, it'll catch up to me eventually. This is proof of that. I take my hand away from my face and look at Oliver.

"I don't work there anymore."

He nods slowly. "Okay...that's...I mean, it would be okay if you still did, but-"

"It's okay, you don't need to explain. It wouldn't be fair of me to lie to you about something like that. But I left there years ago...I took the job at the cafe instead. And the freelance work to cover the loss in money I was making. It was good money back then. That's why I had to do it. But I won't ever go back. And I thought I had escaped all of that. Apparently not."

Oliver nods again, his brow creased. I can read his mind so easily right now. I know he wants to say things that sound supportive. I know he wants to be the guy that tells me it doesn't bother him. But I think it does. It must do. It's like he's dug up some sleazy dirt on me that should've stayed buried. Except I refuse to be ashamed of this.

"Oliver...life hasn't handed me anything at all. At the time, working there was my only option."

He leans forward, ready to listen. I take a deep breath. I know I'm about to tell him things I've never told anybody. But I need to do this. I need to stop keeping everything inside me. I need to stop thinking my secrets can destroy me.

"It was always just me and my Dad...he was an alcoholic. When I was younger, it wasn't so bad...he'd be the kind of happy drunk where he'd want to help me bake cookies at midnight, or let me eat sweets until I felt sick in front of the TV. But when I was twelve, he lost his job. He couldn't find another one...or he didn't bother trying. I'm not sure which, now that I think about it. But everything changed after that. By the time I was thirteen, I was walking three miles to school every day because he didn't have a car. I used to come home with out of date bread that I'd buy with money from his wallet and eat it dry because that's all we could afford. He signed up for benefits, but it barely covered rent...especially when he was drinking so heavily. And I guess one day he just snapped. He was so angry at the way his life had turned out...he just used to be so furious all the time. And I don't know...somewhere along the way, he began blaming me for it. He used to hit me just for breathing."

"Willow…"

There are hot tears streaming down my cheeks. I'm not ashamed to cry. What happened to me makes me sad every day of my life, but it's made me who I am today. I've never let that hold me back. I wipe my eyes even as more tears replace the ones that I just brushed away.

"It hurts. It really does. I watched my Dad become someone else. I don't even know what he's doing now, or where he is…he could be dead in a ditch. He's not my concern now." I sniff. "I hope he's okay…I hope he's found a way to heal. But it's too late for me and him…I sometimes wonder what would've happened if I stayed. I watched him get worse and worse…maybe he would've killed me some day."

"Willow…I'm so sorry. I had no idea."

"No one knows. I always kept it to myself. I moved out at seventeen. I cut most of my ties with people from where I grew up, even though they're still living in the city. Liverpool has always been my home, through the hard times and the good ones…but I felt I had to leave my other reminders of my past behind."

Oliver's hand slips into mine. "I can understand that. My brother…my brother did the same after my Dad died."

I sniff and give him an encouraging smile. "Do you want to talk about that? While we're spilling our souls, you might as well…"

Oliver sighs. "I mean, it's simple really. My parents chose to smoke and drive…Mom crashed the car, but Dad's the one who died. And our family never moved on from that. How could we?"

I can see Oliver chewing the inside of his cheek like he's trying to bite back some of the emotion he's feeling.

"It was a few years ago now…I guess I've come to terms with it. But it destroyed how I thought about them. We were from a wealthy family…they could've done anything they wanted with their lives. Why did they have to go out and get high like dumb teenagers? They were meant to be the grown-ups. The ones who kept us safe and never made bad decisions. I know now, as an adult, that might not be realistic…but they were parents first and foremost. They made a selfish decision…and it's hard to forgive them for that."

I nod, hardly knowing what to say. He's right, of course. They made a bad choice. I squeeze his hand.

"People make mistakes all the time. But they loved you. That's something to hold onto."

Oliver sniffs a little. "But not enough to stop Dad from getting killed. They ripped a hole right down the centre of our home. Caleb's gone now…he won't talk to Mom. Tammy has to stay home just to look after Mom…these are meant to be the best years of her life and she's stuck with Mom because of her bad decisions. And then Ezra...well, I think it hit him the hardest. He's always been emotional...and he couldn't hack the aftermath. He hates seeing us all fight."

"Well...whose side do you take?"

Oliver sighs. "I don't take a side. I keep my distance as much as possible from it all. I don't know what else to do. If I side with Caleb then Tammy will never forgive me. Neither will Mom. But when I try to side with Tammy, Caleb gets all defensive, as though he didn't choose to leave our family behind...it's easier to just accept that I'm stuck somewhere in the middle."

"I mean...I guess that's a good thing in a way...but I can understand how that sucks...not being able to express an opinion."

Oliver looks up at me with a sad smile. "You know...that day when I walked out of class...I felt really alone. I felt like no one would understand how I feel. But you just...you get it, don't you? The things we've been through are so different...but you listen to me long enough to understand. Not many people would do that for me."

I swallow. I feel more nervous being vulnerable like this than I did when we kissed the first time. I've opened up about things I never speak about. Now, sitting here with him, I know why we've connected. We're both a little bit broken, but with hearts full of love to give.

Maybe he can give some of his love to me.

CHAPTER ELEVEN

Oliver

"Are you sure you don't mind me staying?" I ask for the third time. Willow rolls her eyes at me with a smile as she plumps up one of the pillows on her bed. She's still a little red from all the crying, but she seems more relaxed now. Like she's finally got something off her chest.

"I don't mind. It's late, you shouldn't walk home alone. There's plenty of room in my bed."

Technically, there isn't. It's one of those three-quarter sized beds that they make for students when they head off to university. Not a single, but not a double. It's going to be cozy in here…

She doesn't seem to mind that idea, though. She's slipped into an old pair of shorts and a baggy old t-shirt, her blue hair loose and brushed out, looking a little static as a result. I've never seen her this relaxed. She gets under the duvet and wriggles around a little, getting comfy. I stare at her, realizing how much I want to get in beside her and wrap my arms around her. I've never felt such an urge to get close to someone like that. I've also never been so damn horny in my life, and I didn't think that both these feelings could co-exist. I guess Willow just makes me want everything I've never had before.

"Are you coming in or what?" she asks. She's facing the wall so I feel a little less self-conscious as

I take off my jeans and t-shirt. Another new sensation…nervousness. I never got nervous before getting into bed with Violet. Maybe it's because this means something to me. Maybe it's because I'm not sure where the night will head. Or maybe it's because I'm scared I'll mess this up, like I always seem to mess everything up. Especially when it comes to Willow.

But she's asking me to do this. And I want to. So I get in beside her and find that my body feels right next to hers. It curves around her body until we're slotted easily together, my arm over her and my face buried in her hair. I sometimes used to do this with Violet, but my heart never beat as fast as it is doing now. Her hair smells like the red wine we drank before we came to bed. The skin of her arm is soft against mine. I feel like I can barely breathe in her presence. How did I end up lying next to this enigmatic woman, knowing that if I'm lucky she might just let me in a little? We've broken down walls tonight and before she builds hers back up again, I want to make sure I'm on her side of the fence.

I can feel her breathing hard as we lie quietly together. Maybe she's as nervous as I am. She grabs her phone from beside her pillow and begins to type something. I feel a little offended at first, wondering why she's texting while we're doing something like this, but then rain sounds come from her speakers and she slides her phone away again, settling down on her pillow once more.

"I find it relaxing," she whispers. "Sometimes at night when it's loud here I just put them on and it helps me drift off to sleep."

I wonder if sleep is what she's thinking about now. I'm still learning to read this girl. I want to touch her, but I'm not sure if she wants that. We're quiet for a few minutes and then I finally get the confidence to brush her leg gently with my fingertips. She responds with a sigh. Not a dismayed sigh, but a gentle, satisfied one. With her back to me, I can't see her face, but as she backs her body up against me, her ass grinding against me gently, I know she wants this.

But I'm happy to go slowly right now. What's the point in rushing this thing when we have all night? What's the point of diving in head first when this is the first time I actually care about what sex means? I'm hard as hell right now and I could just flip her over and fuck her, the way I've done with other women before, but it doesn't feel right. I follow my instincts, gently caressing her thigh. I place a few tender kisses on her shoulders, buried in the woozy scent of her hair. She's quivering a little beneath my touch. She's not the kind of girl to shy away from a moment of intimacy. I know without asking her that this isn't her first time, and I know she's not exactly shy. But it's like it is for me. It matters to her.

I close my eyes and just savour this moment. Our bodies close together. Our breathing heavy with anticipation, but our bodies relaxed. I find myself pressing against her so she can feel my hardness behind her even more potently. She's still facing the wall, but her hand stretches behind her to touch my leg. It's not a particularly intimate place to be touched, but it sends sparks through my body anyway. Only she seems to be able to make my body react with even the slightest nudge of her hand.

The rain sounds around us divert us from complete silence and I'm glad. The tension between us is already too much without the silence making it harder. I move my hand higher to her hip and rest it there a moment, trying to decide whether I have permission to do the things I want to do to her body. In response, she turns over so I can finally see her face. I see the lust in her eyes. Her lips part and she breathes out slowly, like she's composing herself. Right now, we're holding back, but I sense she's about to give in. And from here, this night is going to go very differently.

She climbs on top of me, our eyes locked. I'm so enthralled that I know I couldn't look away if I tried. She threads her fingers through mine and presses my hands down onto the pillow. I'm at her mercy right now. I'm not used to someone so domineering, but I like it. She shifts herself a little, grinding gently on me through my boxers. Her nipples poke out against the material of her old t-shirt and a small smile plays on her lips. She's nervous, but there's a sparkle in her eyes.

"You know...if we do this...we're all in, okay? Like, we're exclusive to one another," she says, moving closer so her lips are hovering over mine. I chuckle.

"Why would I refuse that when you're turning me on so damn much?" I murmur. She throws back her head as she laughs and I grin back. Seeing her laugh only makes this whole thing hotter. Who wants silent sex when you could have it full of love and laughter?

She presses my hands into the pillow again as she kisses me. I groan against her lips. My cock is throbbing for her. Damn, this is what I've been missing. All this time I could've been here with her…

But we're making up for lost time. Her tongue slides into my mouth and she grinds against me. I've never been this turned on. I must really fucking want this.

I sit up and her legs wrap around my waist. She's sitting right over the top of my cock now and she pulls my face closer to kiss me. Entwined in one another, she moves steadily, working up my appetite for this before we've even removed an item of clothing. I cup her breast, tweaking her stiff nipple through her t-shirt and earning a moan from her lips. I grab the bottom of the t-shirt and pull it over her head. She gets tangled for a moment and the pair of us giggle like teenagers, but the second she escapes, I'm enchanted by the sight of her topless. She arches backward a little so I can clamp my mouth around her nipple as she continues to grind against me. She moans and my hands find her waist, pulling her closer to me. She can't get close enough for my liking.

Part of me is desperate to go wild, to take this to another level, but another part of me wants to savour every single second. I want this to be a romantic experience for her. She deserves it. But as she grinds against me again, I know she's deliberately driving me crazy with lust. She doesn't seem interested in some slow, romantic experience anymore. She grabs one of my hands and puts it between her legs, demanding more. I follow her lead. I want to give her exactly what she asks for.

I move her shorts aside and find that her underwear is soaked wet. She's as turned on as I am. I find her sweet spot through her panties, massaging her clit gently at first. I want to drive her wild. I want to see her really let loose. She moans and the sound is like a drug to me. Knowing she's into this is the biggest turn on I could ever ask for.

She leans in to kiss me as I touch her and my other hand grapples for the back of her neck, pulling her close. I can barely believe that this beautiful woman is here with me. As my lips venture down her neck, she giggles.

"It tickles," she giggles before capturing my lips with hers again. This whole thing feels new to me. Sex has always been so intense and serious for me in the past. This feels impossibly sexy and crazily lighthearted all at once.

I want to get rid of the rest of her clothes. I tug at her shorts, but she's still straddling me. She makes a surprised noise.

"Oh, okay...one second."

She hops off the bed to take off her shorts and her underwear. I shuffle out of my boxers and watch her in awe. As she stands in front of me naked, she takes my breath away. Her curved hips and thick thighs look even better without her clothes covering her up. I just want her back on top of me so we can finish what we started. I want to touch every inch of her beautiful skin. I want to make love to her. I want to show her exactly what she means to me.

"Come back," I tell her, reaching to grab her hips and pull her closer. She leans in to kiss me, taking my cock in her hand and beginning to stroke it up and down.

"As you command," she purrs.

Willow

My past somewhat diminished my views of sex. I always saw it as a means to an end, not an act of intimacy. But here with Oliver, it's different. My body has come alive in ways I never expected. I want this more than I've ever wanted it with anyone else. I'm so turned on by it all that I don't even feel like I need to fake how much I'm into this. And now that both of us are naked, his cock in my hand

and our lips pressed together, I feel a rush inside me, knowing exactly how good this is going to be.

We clamber back onto the bed together as I pleasure him. His hands find my breasts and he pinches my left nipple between his thumb and finger until I groan against his lips. As I'm leaning over him, he encourages me back to my position straddling him and I think for a moment that he wants to go straight to sex, but then his fingers find the wet folds between my legs and he begins to run his fingers over my sex. Then his fingers slide inside me like they were always meant to be there and I moan, allowing him to start finger fucking me as I continue to pleasure him. I find myself grinding against his hand, thrusting him deeper and taking the sensation to another level. My eyes meet his and I can see how much he's enjoying it. As he lies back and watches me on top of him, I can tell he's living out his own personal fantasy. Maybe he's been thinking about this just as much as I have.

I'm used to being a man's fantasy. That's what stripping is all about...showing yourself off, keeping yourself just out of reach as they marvel at your body, craving your assets as you show them what they can't touch. But I don't want to be that to Oliver. I don't want to be his fantasy. I want to be his reality.

"Come closer," he groans as his fingers delve deep inside me. I lean over to kiss his lips, still working his cock.

"Close enough?" I murmur. He shakes his head.

"Nowhere near close enough."

I know exactly what he means. He's done waiting. The foreplay is fun, but we both know what we're really craving. Normally we might take this part slow and enjoy it, but it feels like I've been waiting a lifetime to have him inside me. Now, we don't want to wait any longer.

I find a condom inside my dresser and slide it on over his cock. Then I pull him back up into a sitting position and move myself over his member like before. I want to feel close to him as we do this. As I sink myself down onto him, I moan in pleasure. It's been a while since I did this last, but as I begin to ride him, gripping him hard and holding him close to me, I know this won't be like other times. As we move together, I close my eyes and savour it. His lips press to my neck, peppering my skin in tender kisses. It's both hot as hell and sweet as sugar. His hands clasp my butt and he tilts his head back so that he can look into my eyes. We kiss as we amp up the heat, our bodies finding a new rhythm that's faster, more intense, wilder somehow. I'm a little breathless. This kind of pace is new to me, but I guess I always lacked passion before. With each movement, he goes deeper inside me and it feels so good that I cry out and an orgasm hits me like a tidal wave. I feel dizzy with pleasure and I shudder, breathing hard as I ride it out, savouring every second of it.

But he's far from done with me. He grabs me by my waist and switches the dominance to himself as he tips me off him and lays me on my back. He slides out of me for a moment, but he's back within moments, pulling my legs up around his waist as he enters me again. He thrusts deep inside me and even faster as I'm still trembling from my first orgasm. I lock him in with my legs and he moves his hands up to touch my breasts. We're looking into one another's eyes as he fucks me. I can see that he's getting more confident, loving the look of lust that's written all over my face. He's good and he knows it. I guess he's had the practice, but that doesn't matter. He chose to be here with me now. Our past doesn't matter anymore. Tonight has taught me that more than anything.

Our bodies are one. We're pressed close together and his hands entwine with mine as he continues to go deep inside me. I lean in, desperate to kiss him. Somehow, kissing him is the most intimate act of all. With his mouth on mine, his lips soft yet insistent, I feel closer to him than I've felt to anyone in a very long time.

"You look so beautiful, Willow," he murmurs against my lips. My breath catches in my throat. I've never been called beautiful before. It's not that I've never felt attractive, or that no one has ever appreciated me...but beautiful has never been a word used to describe me. It catches me off guard and tightens my throat. He senses the shift in mood and his movements inside me become slower, more gentle, more loving. He cups my face in his hands and we watch one another for a few moments, our eyes flickering over each other's features. He kisses my neck slowly and gently, his mouth moving to kiss my collarbone.

"So beautiful," he murmurs. I have to hold back tears. I've never felt so special. I know that my worth isn't based on my looks, and I don't need a man to feel good about myself. But his softly spoken words and the gentle way he's changed the course of the sex has made me feel so seen. He's responsive to my feelings. He understands me without me having to say a word. I wrap my arms around his neck and his arms wrap around me. I close my eyes and feel the magic.

This time, the climb to my orgasm is gradual and slow, but it's also tender and my entire body feels sensitive and responsive to his touch. There are gentle caresses of our hands, eye contact that lingers, kisses that give me butterflies in my stomach. I feel like I've run through every emotion since the sex began, but it's always a rollercoaster ride with Oliver. Maybe it always will be. But if it feels this good then who am I to complain?

I feel myself crashing into my second orgasm just as Oliver grunts and finishes too, collapsing against me. Still inside me, he kisses me, his hands gripping me like he doesn't want to let me go. He doesn't want this to be over, and neither do I. But now that we have one another, we don't need to worry that this is the last time. We can have this whenever we want.

He kisses my forehead gently as he slides out of me. "I'll be back...just got to clean up."

I nod, suddenly a little nervous. But when he smiles and kisses my lips, I forget to be scared. For once, I've got something good in my life, and the thought of him slipping away is a hard one to deal with. But he's not going anywhere. He promised me, and I believe him.

At least, I want to.

CHAPTER TWELVE

Oliver

There's a new-found peace inside me today as I walk to university. It's been two days since I saw Willow, but we've been texting back and forth this whole time. Things are easy between us now, like we've been best friends for years. I don't feel any pressure to see her every second of every day, though I wouldn't turn down a single second with her if she had more time. I guess it's because I'm so confident in what we have that I don't feel like we have to constantly prove that to one another. Maybe she doesn't feel the same yet - after all, I'm the one who made this difficult in the first place. I'm the one with making up to do. But I'm determined to show her that I'm serious about this, about *us*. At the same time, I'm trying to play it cool because I don't want to rush this and ruin it before it's even started, but the truth is, I'm in pretty deep at this point.

I've been tossing the idea around in my head of another study session so that we can hang out while she works. It's not a dream date, but if that's all she has time for then I'll happily take it.

But I have this excitement in me, like I want to take her everywhere with me. I have this urge to take her on fancy dates to nice restaurants, to go mini-golfing with her, to snuggle in cinemas with her, to dance all night with her beside me in my favorite clubs. I want to take her on city breaks and explore new places together, then show her all my comforting, familiar places around town. All the things that Violet was trying to encourage me to do with her...and I want to do them with another woman.

Knowing I'll have to face her today is hard. I know how much I've hurt her and it'll hurt even more when I opt to sit with Willow in the lecture hall today. I don't know if our friendship can recover from this anymore. I'm angry with her too for trying to sabotage my relationship with Willow, but I guess that's my fault in the first place. People make mistakes that they can't go back on, and this was mine. Now I have to deal with the consequences.

But I can't help feeling like it was worth it for Willow. I have ten minutes until class, and I know she's finishing up a shift at the coffee shop beforehand, so I decide to drop by. Seeing her standing behind the counter in her apron, I feel a smile forming on my face. She looks up and smiles at me, looking slightly shy as she tucks a strand of hair behind her ear.

"Hey. Coffee?" she asks. I smile.

"Nah. Just wanted to come and say hello," I say. I slip a fiver out of my pocket and into the tips jar. "And say that I had absolutely awesome service today."

She rolls her eyes, but she's smiling. "I know I told you the tips are bad here, but you don't need to make up for shitty customers."

I lean across the counter with a smile, waggling my eyebrows at her. "Oh, I'm not giving that up for free. I expect a kiss."

She flicks a packet of sugar at me in response and I laugh, backing off. "Alright, alright, I hear you. No PDA. But hey...I'm saving you a seat in class."

Her eyes soften. "You don't have to sit with me, Oliver. You've got your own friends...and maybe you should be trying to patch things up with Violet."

"After class. This is the only chance I'll get to see you today...I'm not wasting it."

Her cheeks are red. From what she's told me, she's never had a steady guy before. We haven't discussed what we are yet, except for the fact that we won't be seeing other people, but I'm working up to asking her to be my girlfriend. Maybe it's premature, but this feels right, and I want her to know I'm serious. It's been years since I felt this good, and that's all down to her. And seeing her smile, I want it even more.

"Okay...save me a seat. I won't be long," she says. Before she can stop me, I lean right over the counter and peck her cheek before rushing away.

"You'll pay for that!" she shouts after me, but I know she's laughing. My cheeks hurt from grinning.

This is how it should be. This is what I've been waiting for.

My phone buzzes in my pocket and I take it out with a smile. It's Tammy.

Still on cloud nine?

I'm higher than the clouds, I text back. *I'm in heaven. Nah, scrap that. Somewhere better than heaven.*

Damn. Throw me a ladder? I'm still stuck in hell.

Can't, it'll go up in flames.

You're the worst brother ever.

I head downstairs to my lecture hall, still smiling to myself. Nothing can touch me today, I'm sure of it. Not even Violet if she's got an attitude. Not even my other friends, who no doubt have heard about me and Willow and have taken Violet's side since I haven't heard from them in days. Not even the thought that I spent three years building connections here and now I have none can bring me down.

The lecturer hasn't shown up yet, but most of my friends are crowded in the lecture hall, looking at something on Hugo's phone. I'm prepared to roll my eyes at whatever it is. He's always been the class clown, and clearly, he's got everyone riled up over something. They're all laughing raucously as though it's the funniest thing on Earth. I have to admit I'm curious what they're looking at. I approach tentatively. These are still supposed to be my friends, after all.

"What are you looking at?" I ask, shifting my bag on my shoulder awkwardly. Hugo splutters with laughter, setting the others off. I start to get an intense feeling of discomfort and I almost wish I hadn't asked. I've got a bad feeling about this.

"Check it out. Your new girlfriend is the talk of the town," Hugo grins, showing me his phone. My heart stops.

The picture of Willow from the strip club is on his phone. I shake my head, willing the image to go away. Not because it matters what her job used to be, but because now that other people know about this, everything is going to change for Willow. This shouldn't be public knowledge unless she wants it to be. How the hell did this get out? I know Rob and whoever was on his birthday night out saw these pictures, but they'd have no reason to share them around so callously. So who?

I look at Violet and know immediately that something is amiss. She's not laughing with the others. She won't look in my direction. This has to be her doing. Her way of getting back at me. I feel my heart sinking to my stomach. I never thought my best friend would stoop this low. I guess this whole time I've been pretty oblivious to her true colours. Was it not enough for her to try and break me and Willow apart, to make me question Willow? Did she really have to dig deeper for satisfaction?

"Stop looking at those pictures," I snap. "She's going to be here soon."

Hugo tuts, rolling his eyes. "Chill out, Oliver. We don't want to look at pictures of your girlfriend half naked. Damn, who does? Really thought you had better taste, man."

I have to hold myself off from attacking him. If I get in a fight right now, I'll get into trouble and the university will get involved. They'll want to know why I beat that asshole senseless and I'll have to expose Willow's secret even more. I'm ending this here.

"Delete it. Right now."

Hugo cocks his head at me. "I can't delete it, man. It's on the internet for everyone to see. It's a free country...anyone can look at it. Does that make you uncomfortable?"

I could punch him. Hugo has always walked the line between being entertaining and being an asshole. I watch as he snakes his arm around Violet's waist and I grit my teeth. Now I see why he's got it out for me. He's Violet's rebound and he knows it. This shit is more personal than I thought. I have to switch tactics. I hold out my hand for the phone.

"Please, Hugo. Stop this now. I'll do whatever you want. I don't want to drag her into this. She doesn't deserve it."

No one is laughing now, but Hugo is still smirking. I guess no one expected the joke to go this far.

"Nah. I don't think I've had my fun with this yet. Hey look...here she comes now."

I feel sick as I turn to see Willow walking toward the door through its clear glass window. She's smiling, a spring in her step. I turn back to Hugo.

"Don't you fucking dare…"

The door opens and the room is silent. I turn and see Willow's face turn from happiness to confusion and nervousness. Hugo leaps to his feet, ready to launch his next attack.

"Give us a dance then, Willow," Hugo bolsters, miming dancing on a pole graphically. Willow's mouth falls open as a few people chuckle quietly, simultaneously mildly amused and wholly uncomfortable. They're so concerned about protecting their status in the group that they refuse not to laugh at the cheap shot.

But Willow stumbles back like she's been shot in the stomach. I feel the blow as she does; the anxiety, the shock, the unfairness of it all. She thought it was behind her and now everyone knows about her past.

Her eyes fall on me.

Hurt fills her eyes. She thinks I did this. My mouth falls open, but I can't find any words to say. I'm glued to the ground, unable to move. I watch as she shakes her head to herself and exits the way she just came, rushing toward the stairs.

No one is laughing now. I finally manage to move, turning to the group of silent onlookers.

"I hope you're fucking happy with where your cheap joke got you," I spit at Hugo. My eyes find Violet and I want to tell her how angry she's made me, but the words stick in my throat like they're coated in tar. I choke on my own anger. I don't have time for it. They don't matter. These bastards don't matter at all. I have to find Willow and make sure she's okay.

I run from the lecture hall, barrelling past my tutor as I make for the stairs. He calls after me, but I'm gone in a flash. I don't care about missing class right now. I just want to make this right. But when I get to the top of the stairs and scout the area, she's already gone.

Willow

I don't want to talk to anyone. I especially don't want to talk to Oliver. I don't know if he told a friend about the website or whether one of his friends leaked it, but he was there with them. Maybe he had a part in it, I don't know. But I'll never live this down now. The rumours about me will spread like wildfire. A guy like Hugo…people might not like him much, but they listen to him. Who cares about my story when he can make one of his own up for me?

I bury my face into my pillow the second I arrive back at my flat and scream into it. I thought I was finally getting somewhere. I thought maybe I might be able to make some friends, have a nice guy to spend time with in my final year of uni and focus on being a young woman for a while. But who is going to take me seriously now? Everyone has this new perception of me that I won't be able to shake. With the brand of a stripper comes so many assumptions about my personality; slut, sex-obsessed, kinky, unfaithful, promiscuous, damaged, broken little Willow. And yet at the same time I'm untouchable, bulletproof, hardened on the inside. Because don't strippers learn somewhere just to let the shots fired at them ricochet off their thickened skin? Don't they learn how to swallow tears and become money hoarding bitches who use their job to make men seem weak and feeble?

I know every stereotype of strippers. I've faced them all from my old customers. They never quite saw me as a real human being. When Hugo looked at me today, I saw exactly what he thought of me. He saw me as beneath him, but he also saw a woman who'd climb on top of him. He made the assumption that I'm begging for it, that my profession was a way to fulfill some gaping hole inside me, some hidden desire to make my life all about sex. And even if that were the case, which it isn't, why should that be his damn business? Why should he get to look at me like I'm nothing more than a sexual object and then claim that I'm the one who is sex obsessed?

I want to cry. I never want to go back there again. People will talk about this. Not forever, but it'll feel like it. I'll have to sit classes with my head hung low and people will assume they know more about me than they ever will. I'll have to act like I'm ashamed of my past.

But I'm not. I never will be. It's part of me and it always will be. Maybe things would've been different if I'd had a supportive family, or if I'd found a different job sooner, but the fact is, my life panned out this way for a reason. Why should I have to be the one who is ashamed? Why shouldn't the people who are talking about me like they have a claim to who I am be the ones blushing to themselves now, thinking about how callously they tried to tear down someone they don't even know?

I sit up and force myself to breathe. *In. Out. In. Out.* I'm not wasting another tear on this. These emotions should be fuelling me to write. To write something that's going to blow everyone in my class out of the water. Something raw and emotional to show that what sets me apart isn't my past. It's my talent. When I submit my piece for the university magazine, not one person is going to make fun of me.

But before then, I have some scores to settle. My hands are shaking as I pick up my phone. I don't have many of my classmates on social media, but I'm sure the ones I do have will spread the word. I take a deep breath as I focus the camera on myself and go live. A few nosy people begin watching right away. I see Oliver's name pop up at the bottom of my screen. He's watching too.

"I just want to get a few things straight," I say firmly. "I know there are some things being said about me around uni. I know a particular photo is doing the rounds. Fine. I don't care at this point. I don't even care who found it and told people about it. But you should know, all of you who were laughing at me, joking about it, getting some mileage out of my past...I'm not fucking ashamed. I refuse to be ashamed of the job that kept me off the streets when I was eighteen. I'm not ashamed of the fact that I worked in that industry because it's not a shameful act. And I'm not ashamed that I made more in tips than any of you will ever make at your bar jobs now. No disrespect to you either, because that's an honest living. However we choose to keep ourselves going should be our business and our business alone."

I keep thinking that maybe my rant is over, but now that I've started, I can't seem to stop. The amount of people watching this is growing. The pressure is on, but maybe this is the perfect time to show people what I'm made of.

"The industry I worked in wouldn't survive without people paying into it. So before you judge me, how about you take a step back and ask yourself what you'd do without people like me in the world? Those of you that frequent strip clubs and watch porn and follow nude models on social media. And if you think it's funny to laugh at me because I'm plus-sized and in an industry that celebrates thin bodies, then just know that plenty of men were throwing money at my feet. So if you think I'm ugly, that's fine. I like who I am, and so do plenty of other people. You can show your friends those pictures of me all you like and you can laugh because I don't look the same as you. But this body paid for me to get to university. It paid for me to eat and have a bed to sleep in. It paid for me to start working toward a life where I don't have to strip to earn my keep and I can do what I'm best at; writing. And now that I've got this far, it's going to be me reaping the rewards. So keep laughing. When I fill my spot in the student magazine, there won't be a shred of doubt in my mind that I deserve it because I worked my ass off for this. Good luck to the rest of you who seem more concerned with my life than getting on with your own and making something of yourselves. I think I'm the real winner here."

I switch off the camera and take a deep breath. My phone is pinging with notifications, but I switch it off right away. I don't need to hear any more. I've said my bit.

Now it's time to take a deep breath and move the hell on.

CHAPTER THIRTEEN

Oliver

I headed home straight after leaving the lecture. I didn't want to chase Willow down if she wanted a chance to be alone. Then, after seeing her live video, I know I made the right decision. She needs space to process this whole mess. The last thing she probably wants is me muscling in.

But it's been twenty-four hours since then and I've spent every single one of those hours awake, wondering what my next move is. I don't know whether to give her even more space or to go to her and comfort her. For a moment, I considered sending her flowers to cheer her up, but I immediately decided against it. I don't think she's the sort of person who has much use for flowers. I think she'd see them as a waste of money and an empty gesture after the embarrassment she went through. She doesn't want flowers, she wants an apology.

I don't even know if I'm supposed to be apologizing. Violet certainly should be, but I didn't tell a soul about the photographs. I hope Willow knows that, but given our rocky start, I'm not sure how much she trusts me. I can't blame her for that, but now I have no idea how to approach this.

I feel sleep deprived and alone. None of my friends are talking to me, though the only person I really want to speak to is Willow. Even my siblings have been eerily quiet and I don't want to break the silence with more of my problems. I got myself into this...I need to be mature and sort it out for myself.

I pick up my phone and begin to type in our course group chat. I don't know how to speak to Willow, so maybe I should just address the world and see what happens. I want her to know that I had no part in what happened. I want her to know that I support her and I'm not afraid to admit it aloud. Still, I'm scared to message her and get no response, so maybe this has to be the happy medium.

I just want to speak up about the events that have happened recently at uni, I begin. *I don't know exactly what happened or why, and I'm not mentioning any names at the risk of spreading more bullshit. All I'm going to say is that whoever thought it was okay to make our classmate uncomfortable by spreading that image of her should be ashamed of themselves. As she mentioned in her video, she herself has no reason to feel embarrassed. However, for someone to deliberately spread around those pictures with the intent of hurting her is disgusting. I've always felt like our course is an inclusive and friendly bunch of people, but this seems to suggest otherwise.*

Whoever it was who shared the image around, put yourself in the other person's shoes. Consider how you'd feel if it happened to you. And then when you're feeling suitably sorry, go and make a real apology to her. You owe her that much.

To the classmate involved...I'm sorry that this happened to you and I hope you know that I've got your back no matter what. You deserve so much better than this, and I hope I can somehow make it up to you. I promise I'll do whatever it takes to make this better.

I take a deep breath before I press send. I know that it won't be popular with some of my classmates, but I'm past caring. Willow deserves to know that she's got someone who cares about her, even when it seems like she's alone. I think of the things she told me about her father and it makes the whole thing sting more. How could anyone want to hurt her when she's done nothing wrong? How can everyone be so blind to how their laughter hurts, to how it affects someone who hasn't felt love in so long?

That ends now. I take a deep breath and stand up, pacing my room. I'm working up the courage to go over and see her. I know she's not working today so I can bet she's sitting in her apartment, mulling this whole thing over. She's probably not thinking of me - after all she has much more on her mind than whatever this thing between us is - but I can't get her out of my head. I want her to know that. I want her to know that she's my one and only focus now.

I hear the buzzer of my flat go off and I jump. Surely it can't be Willow? The thought that it could be excites me, but I push that thought away as I head to answer it. She's not the kind of girl to come running when she doesn't need to. I answer the buzzer.

"Oliver? Can you let me in?"

Violet. I should've known. I grit my teeth.

"I don't think so."

"It was me…I'm the reason that the image spread around."

"I was already ninety percent sure of that fact, Violet."

"Oliver…please let me explain."

"I'm not the one you owe an explanation to," I say, grabbing my keys. "We're going over to see Willow. You can make your excuses to her."

Before she can protest, I'm already heading downstairs to meet her. When I step out into the street, she doesn't look like herself. She's wearing no makeup and she's in her scruffiest sweatpants. Her hair's a mess and she's not wearing the radiant smile she usually has. I guess these past few weeks have been rough on her.

"Don't give me those puppy dog eyes. I'm not going to feel sorry for you," I scold her, heading off in the direction of Willow's flat without waiting for Violet. She scurries to keep up with me.

"I only showed one person, I swear."

"Yeah? And that person just had to be Hugo didn't it? The kind of guy who'd use that image for his own mileage. Honestly, Violet, what were you thinking?"

"I…I wasn't thinking," Violet mutters. "Well, I guess I was thinking about how to get back at you.

That's why I've been sleeping...hanging out with Hugo in the first place." She pauses, her short legs struggling to keep up with my stride. "Are you...are you angry with me?"

"Yes, Violet, I'm angry with you. And at this point, I think my anger with you surpasses any anger you feel for me. But we all make mistakes, myself more than anyone. That's why we're going to fix it together." I sigh. "Especially since I can't fix what I did to you."

Violet seems small to me now as she shoves her hands into her pockets. "You know...you made it pretty clear all along that you didn't feel the same as me. I just didn't want to admit that to myself. And I know that you didn't have a clue that I wanted you differently...all our friends say how clueless you are all the time."

I manage a small smile. "Yep. That's me."

Violet chews her lip, wavering between a smile and the verge of tears. "I am sorry. I really am."

"I know you are."

"I want Willow to know that too. Do you think...do you think she'll be angry with me?"

I sigh, kicking a can out of my way as I walk. "Maybe at first. But you're lucky, actually. Because Willow is the most forgiving person I've ever met. Not that we deserve that, but hopefully she'll give it to us anyway. She will at least hear us out."

"I can see why you like her."

I feel my cheeks heat up. "Yeah, I do. But I don't know if this whole thing has messed it up...we've had a bumpy start to our relationship."

"Relationship?"

Damn it. For a writer, I always seem to use the wrong words. I rake a hand through my hair. "Not relationship...but whatever we share. You know what I mean. Things keep getting in the way."

"You mean *I* keep getting in the way."

I press my lips together to stop myself from agreeing with her. Violet sniffs.

"Well, you don't need to worry about that anymore. I'll stay out of your way."

There's an aching inside my chest. I want to tell her that we can move past all this. I want to tell her that we can be friends again. But I'm not sure that's true yet. Time will tell. I want her back in my life, but not if it costs me Willow. This whole thing has made me realise I'm actually willing to sacrifice quite a lot if it means that I get my shot with her. But the fact that Violet is sorry is a step in the right direction. Maybe someday we'll get back on the same page.

We're quiet until we reach Willow's flat. I can see Violet glancing around at Willow's neighborhood, taking it in the way I did when I first came here. Realizing that Willow's world differs from ours. Seeing this place, maybe Violet can begin to understand why what she did was so harsh. Willow worked so hard to get to this point and now that's been thrown back in her face. But if Violet's ready to make a real apology, I hope that Willow's ready to accept it too. Then we can put all of this behind us.

"Are you ready?" I ask Violet. She clasps her hands together in front of her and nods nervously. I can tell she'd rather be anywhere else, somewhere far away from me and especially for Willow. But this is needed.

I ring Willow's phone.

Willow

I jump as my phone rings beside me and I see that it's Oliver. I allow myself a small smile. I've been wondering how long it would take him to come to me. I just saw his post about what happened and it erased any doubts I had left about him. I know now that I don't need to be quite so cautious about him. But that doesn't mean I'm going to fall straight into his arms. I'm interested to see how he handles this. I think it'll tell me a lot about the man I've taken such an interest in.

I pick up the phone and answer.

"Hey," I say gently.

"Hi," he says tentatively. He seems nervous. "I'm outside…and there's someone else here who wants to talk to you."

I frown. It's not like I get many visitors here. I head for the door.

"I'm coming to let you in."

When I open the door for Oliver and smile at him, he looks relieved. But my smile fades when I see who he's brought with him. I press my lips together.

"Hi, Violet. Would you like to come in?" I ask. She shifts from foot to foot. It feels like she'd rather be anywhere else.

"Sure, if you don't mind."

"Shall I make a round of tea?" I ask as they both step inside. I'm trying to ignore the obvious awkwardness in the air. Oliver clears his throat.

"How about I make it? You two can talk."

I suddenly know why she's here. She's not here to mend the broken bridges she made with me and Oliver. She's here to tell me that she showed Hugo the pictures. I sigh. Now that I've had some time to process the whole thing, it seems obvious that this is down to her.

"Okay. Violet, why don't we go in my room?"

I don't watch her as she enters the flat. I don't want to see her looking around, judging this life I've built, making assumptions on the limited information she has about me. Still, a blush rests on my cheeks as I lead her to the bedroom.

I shut the door behind us and she sits on the edge of my bed, her face red. My own cheeks heat a little as I remember what happened between Oliver and me here the other day. Now his ex is sitting on my bed and I'm praying that this conversation will be quick and easy.

"I...I have to confess something," Violet says, unable to meet my eyes. "I showed the photo to Hugo. I didn't know that he'd show anyone else...I guess I was trying to get back at you because...well, you have what I want."

I fold my arms across my chest, feeling uncomfortable. I find that I'm not angry at her. More than anything, I feel sorry for her. Unrequited feelings suck. Plus, she's made an idiot of herself. It suddenly doesn't feel like I'm the one who has suffered here.

"I'm sorry that I did it," she adds, almost as an afterthought. "I wasn't always like this, you know. I used to be nice. Or at least I thought I was. This thing has made me feel so...so bitter." She glances at me quickly before looking away again. "And I guess some part of me thought that I was better than you. More deserving of the things I wanted." She shakes her head to herself, looking pained. "I'm definitely not as nice as I thought."

"Look...I get it. I knew from the second we showed up at that party why you didn't like me," I tell her. "I mean...I'm sure we have some things in common, given that we share a university course...and an interest in Oliver. I think we could've been friends. But you sort of threw that idea in my face."

She hangs her head. "I know."

"I get it. Honestly, I do. But this has just turned into a mess now. And you hurt me with what you did."

She nods, still not looking at me. I don't want to make her feel guilty for this. I'm just trying to be honest about what this has done to me. But where's the sense in holding onto this forever? At the end of the day, I have to move on. I have to find peace when my life has been so full of pain. I sit down beside her.

"But that doesn't mean we can't start again."

Violet looks up at me, her eyes swimming with tears.

"Huh?"

I shrug. "You're Oliver's best friend for a reason. I don't want to stand in the way of that. I can forgive the past. Shit happens. I'm alright with putting everything behind us, so long as you mean what you said. What do you think?"

Violet stares at me for a long while. I don't think she can figure out what I want, but that's the thing. I don't want anything. I've got everything I need. I just want to live a perfectly ordinary, perfectly boring life. No more drama. No more arguing over ridiculous things. And more importantly, I want Oliver to be happy. If that means having Violet in his life, then I want her here.

"I don't think I can do it," Violet chokes out. She stands up. "I really appreciate you saying that...but I can't be around either of you right now. It just...it hurts seeing him with someone else. And...I never hated you. I hated myself for not being able to let go of him. I hated myself for not being enough for him." She laughs to herself. "Look at me. I came here to apologise and I'm making this about me." She sniffs, wiping her eyes. I pick up my tissue box from my bedside table and offer her one. She takes one with a grateful smile and blots her eyes delicately.

"Thanks...and I'm sorry."

"It's okay."

"Why are you being so nice to me?" she asks, blowing her nose noisily. I shrug uncomfortably.

"I just...I don't want to make this worse than it already is. And I can see you're sorry. Getting some balance back would be good."

"You're not wrong," Violet snuffles. "Which is why I'm going to go."

I nod in understanding. She takes a deep breath and then looks up at me.

"You know...I don't think we're similar at all," Violet says quietly. "I think I brought out the worst in Oliver. He's changed a lot since you two started talking and…well, he's better off for it. You...you're going to be good for him. I'm really sorry again, Willow. I'll see you in class."

I let her leave without another word. There's nothing more we need to say. She scurries out of the flat without saying goodbye to Oliver, who is at the kitchen counter about to make the tea. He looks anxious as his eyes meet mine.

"Was it okay?"

"It was fine. It went as well as it could've," I say, crossing the room. Instinctively, I wrap my arms around him to hug him close. Suddenly, I'm not interested in holding back or making him fight for a response from me. That's Violet's game, not mine. He seems surprised, but he hugs me back.

"It's good to see you. I was wondering when you'd call," I tell him, breathing him in. Something about the way we're holding each other feels so right. I feel him exhale and I can tell he's been carrying the weight of all this on his shoulders, maybe even more than I have.

"I didn't know if you wanted to hear from me…I thought maybe you needed space. I'm still learning you…I should've come sooner. But I didn't want to mess things up. I haven't, have I? Messed it up?"

"Oliver…"

"I don't want to lose you, Willow. I know that this is only the start, that maybe I shouldn't be in so deep, but I care about you. More than I care about anything else in the world. And I keep fucking it up. I keep trying to write our story one way and it's like I've lost control of the plot. I never wanted any of this to happen."

"I know."

"I hate knowing that people hurt you because of me."

"I know."

Oliver runs a hand through his hair, his eyes full of nerves.

"I know I might not deserve it…but I just need one more chance to get this right, if you're willing. This is just the first draft of you and me, Willow. It's full of mistakes and nothing is going to plan, but I want to work on it. I want to make us a masterpiece. I want it to be me and you on the final page. But only if you want this. Am I…am I too late? Have I messed up too many times?"

I realize as he says it that Oliver isn't a cocksure as he always comes across. He's still learning about me and I'm still learning about him. How can I hold it against him when I can tell that he's spent the past few days agonizing over this? I reach out and touch his face gently.

"It's okay, Oliver. You did everything right. You stuck up for me, and that means the world to me. Neither of us could've seen this coming. And I feel the same way about you. I want this to work. I want…I want to be with you."

Oliver's shoulders relax a little. "So we're okay? You're not mad at me?"

I pull away for a moment. "Oliver…there was a moment where I thought maybe you were involved in the picture getting out. Then there was a moment where I considered that maybe it was your fault because of the things that happened between you and Violet. But then I really thought about it and I realised that you're the one person who has had my back. Ever. You've made mistakes, but I'm okay with that. Everyone does sometimes. I really want this to work. Even if it's a bumpy ride…it's one I want to take." I look him deeply in the eyes. "Let's just scrap the first draft, yeah? Start over again from page one. Make new mistakes and rewrite them together. Whatever metaphor you want to use…I'm in."

Oliver smiles, his eyes filled with emotion. "Me too. Willow...I…"

He reaches out to touch my cheek, but he doesn't finish his sentence. I grin.

"Have words escaped the wordsmith?"

He grins. "Shut up."

"Only if you kiss me."

He does as I ask. Our lips connect and I feel hope rise inside me. Hope that this might be something good. Hope that we're not going to screw this up now. Hope that we're past all the uncertainty, the fighting, the nervousness and the bad decisions.

Hope that that I might finally have some luck.

EPILOGUE

Three months later...

Oliver

The grass is a little damp as I lay out the picnic blanket at Sefton Park. I've chosen one of Willow's favorite spots, right close to the fountain and the ice cream shop. She's managed to wrangle the day off so that we can have this date before the launch of the university magazine later tonight. It's the perfect opportunity to make her feel special for the day. The sun is shining, even if it is a little cold, and the park is quiet and serene. Willow is going to love this when she shows up.

I've sent her a text to tell her where to meet me. I unpack the picnic I've made that includes all of her favorite foods and a bottle of rose wine. I made sure not to go crazy with the expense. I know that Willow can be sensitive about money, especially considering that all of my debts were paid off by my brother. But starting this week, all that is changing. I'm beginning my job at the same cafe she works at to begin the process of paying my brother back. I'll be taking out a loan for my master's degree next semester like the majority of students, and I'll have to pay it off myself, with interest, like everyone else. I'm moving out of my expensive flat and I'll be moving somewhere more affordable. But that's the part I haven't told Willow yet. That's the part I'm saving for this picnic.

When she shows up, she takes my breath away as usual. She's wearing short dungarees that show off her thick thighs and her luscious hips. Her blue hair has been woven into a crown on her head and her face is clear of makeup. She looks so beautiful that I have to take a second to remind myself that she's mine. And now that I have her, I'll do pretty much anything to keep her at my side.

"This is so sweet," she says as she examines the picnic blanket. "And wine at lunchtime? It makes me feel like an adult…"

"Well, I guess we are adults now," I say as she sits down beside me. "University is pretty much over…after the showcase tonight, all we have left is graduation and results day."

"And then another two years of classes for our masters degree," Willow laughs. I smile. I'll admit, I was torn about taking the master's degree. Another two years of studying seems like a lot, especially when all I've done is complain about the workload since I started uni. But Willow was set on doing it, and I'm not ready to head back to America, especially if she won't be coming too. Besides, a master's degree will at least set me apart from other students. Losing a spot in the magazine this year really humbled me, even though I was ridiculously happy for Willow. She deserved it more than anyone, but I guess it means I have to work harder to stand out when she shines so damn bright next to me.

"It's going to be worth it to spend another few years in this city…with you," I tell her. She smiles and leans in to kiss me.

"You're sweet."

I grin. "Well, I'm glad you think so…because I have something to ask you. It'll definitely go down better if I'm in your good books."

Willow takes one of the plastic cups from the picnic basket and begins to pour herself a glass of wine. "Uh oh…I get the feeling I need a drink in my hand for this."

I laugh. "It's nothing bad, I swear…I just think it makes sense."

"Go on then. I'm listening."

She takes a sip of wine and I breathe in. This is it. I slide my hand into hers and she brushes her thumb over my knuckle. It relaxes me a little.

"Okay, so…we've been dating a while now…we spend basically all our time together, at my place or at yours…and now that we know we're going to be staying in the same city for the next few years…well, I just figured…I could use a roommate."

Willow grins at me, sipping her wine with a raised eyebrow. She can tell I'm struggling talking about this. "A roommate, hmm? So you're looking for a buddy to live with?"

I sigh, rolling my eyes with a smile. "You know what I'm asking. I want to live with you, Willow. Not just because it makes sense to split rent with someone...but because I want to spend all my time with you if I can."

"What, going to classes together and being co-workers isn't going to be enough for you?" she teases.

"Not even close...I know I sound clingy, but when I'm with you...I'm just happier. Happier than I have been in a really long time," I tell her honestly. I don't talk this honestly very often, but I want her to know how I really feel. When it comes to her, she's perfect. She feels like home already, but now I want to share a home with her for real.

Willow chews her lip. Then she smiles. "You know what? If someone had told me that I'd say yes to moving in with a boy I've only been dating for a few months last year...I wouldn't have believed them. You know how careful I am, Oliver. I'm not exactly impulsive. But I do trust my gut...and my gut is telling me that this is a good decision. So yes...I'll move in with you."

I grin so hard that my cheeks hurt. Willow smiles back, cupping my cheeks as she leans in to kiss me. She tastes sweet from the wine and it only lifts my soul even more. She's right. This feels so perfect. When she pulls away, her cheeks are flushed and she picks her wine back up.

"Wow. I guess we really are celebrating then."

"We already were," I tell her, pouring myself a cup of wine and raising it to her. "I want to toast to you...to you making it into the top spot in the magazine. To you acing all of your coursework and presentations while balancing two jobs and a needy boyfriend...to you being absolutely perfect. To you, Willow."

"To us," she murmurs. "Always to us."

I hesitate for a moment. I know what I want to say to her, but once again, words fail the wordsmith. I shift a little closer to her, my anxiety clawing at my stomach. But Willow is smiling, her eyes a little heavy with something between bliss and ease.

"I love you, Oliver," she whispers. Her words take a moment to sink in. She's caught me off guard. But I look in her eyes and I know she means it. And all of the anxiety suddenly melts away.

"You stole the words right out of my mouth."

"You can still say them," she teases. I take a deep breath, slipping my hand into hers.

"I love you. I've loved you right from the start. And I'm going to keep on loving you for as long as you'll let me."

Willow smiles.

"I will always let you love me, Oliver. And I'll always love you right back."

Willow

The pub is loud and intimidating as I stand at the front of the room by the microphone, ready for my reading. As the winner of the prime spot in the magazine, it's compulsory for me to read out a snippet of the story I wrote. I close my eyes with a small smile and remember all the things that inspired it. My new found relationship with Oliver. The darkness of my past. My time as a stripper. My life has been far from conventional, and my work has always reflected it. But standing up here in front of all my classmates, ready to let them see all my scars, is pretty damn scary.

It's even more terrifying when I see who is sitting right at the front of the room. On one side is Oliver and a few of our closest friends, waiting eagerly for me to speak. They're the scariest bunch to perform for. I feel like if it goes wrong, I'll be a disappointment to them. They're here for me and I don't want to get it wrong when they're desperate to support me.

And then on the other side, there's Violet. I haven't seen her much these past few months. I think she's been avoiding lectures, trying not to show her face. But she's here tonight and when I look her way, our eyes lock together. She offers me the smallest smile and some of my fear about seeing her fades away. I wave to her and just like that, none of what happened between us matters to me anymore. Sure, it hurt at the time. Sure, she tried her hardest to make sure me and Oliver wouldn't get a happy ending. But I got everything I wanted. I moved on and I'm sure she has done too. I think that's why she's here. It's the end of our final year, the end of everything we've spent three years building up to. It's the end of an era and the start of a new beginning. I don't need to hold on to any of it...except for Oliver.

But standing in the way of me and my future is this reading. This damned speech. I came here to be a writer, not a public speaker, but it's also customary for the person who takes the prime spot in the magazine to make a speech about their time at the university before they do their reading. I clear my throat, ready to begin. I want to get this over with, really. Everyone's eyes turn to me and I take a deep breath.

"Hi, everyone. I'm honoured to be standing here as both a student of this university and as a writer in the university magazine," I begin. "This year has been one of the most challenging...most rewarding...*best* years of my life. I started this journey feeling like I was alone. I felt overwhelmed by my own life. And now, through this course...through the friends I've made along the way...from my own resilience, I've found happiness that I never thought would be in my reach. And that's why I'm humbled to be standing here in front of you all, ending this year on a high note."

There's a light spattering of applause around the room and I pause with a smile. Oliver is leading the way, clapping hard for me. I can barely believe that we're going to be moving in together. It feels like everything has suddenly fallen into my lap. I have everything I could want. As I look out at the room, I recall that there were people in here happy to see me fail. I remind myself that they're not all my friends. But even though this moment in time feels so important right now, it's just a pinpoint in our long timelines. What's the point in being bitter when this will all be behind us soon? I smile at the room. It's time to just enjoy myself. This is my night. I earned it. It's time to show them that.

"I'm surrounded by so many talented people in this room and so many people deserved the top spot. But I can't pretend that it means nothing to me to be selected, because it means everything. It's a testament to how hard work and patience can take you wherever you want to go. Next year, someone else will stand here and feel this. Next year, someone in this room will accept their dream job, or get married to the love of their life, or travel to the one place they've always dreamed of seeing. Success comes when you least expect it...and yes, life can be tough sometimes. But moments like this remind me that the world has something good in store for everyone. No matter your struggle, no matter how much time it takes...it's worth it in the end. Thank you for listening, I hope you enjoy my reading."

As I finish my speech with a smile, the room breaks out into applause properly this time. Some people stand to applaud and I blush, ducking my head for a moment. But then I see Oliver smiling at me and I lift up my chin. He's my reminder that I've made it. I've found happiness. I've found hope. I've found love.

It's time to hold my head high and embrace it.

THE END